DANIEL SANTOS

GRAVE OF
LOST DREAMS

Contents

1.	Chapter 1	1
2.	Chapter 2	10
3.	Chapter 3	15
4.	Chapter 4	19
5.	Chapter 5	23
6.	Chapter 6	29
7.	Chapter 7	36
8.	Chapter 8	41
9.	Chapter 9	49
10.	Chapter 10	64
11.	Chapter 11	76
12.	Chapter 12	86
13.	Chapter 13	101
14.	Chapter 14	108

15. Chapter 15   117

16. Chapter 16   131

17. Chapter 17   147

18. Chapter 18   162

19. Chapter 19   180

20. Chapter 20   184

21. Chapter 21   191

22. Chapter 22   194

23. Chapter 23   201

Chapter 1

Sofia's body jiggled in her seat. Just like last week and the week before, her mother took the time to drive her to Dr. Hoffman's office. Yet, each time she did so, Sofia always gave her side glances. All she could remember during her upbringing was her mother raising her voice. So, why was she trying so hard to help her? Maybe she only saw Sofia as a flawed human being. An unhinged daughter.

"How are you feeling?" her mom asked.

Sofia scoffed and placed her feet on the dashboard—a pose that reminded her of her father. His calm demeanor imprinted itself in her mind. Her eyes ran over the old, beat-up tennis shoes he gave her. Now, they served as a reminder of her past life. A life before her mother divorced him.

She really wanted to see his face. She willed the few happy memories that remained to surface. However, the immense amount of mental strain it left on her was more exhausting than being on the track team. But in the few attempts she successfully recalled those days, she savored those memories for as long as she could. Just seeing her dad grabbing those shoes off the shelf while her mother protested prompted a smile to come out. *Stop! Those are fifty dollars!* Sofia chuckled to herself when she recalled her reaction. Unlike her mother, her father always found joy. He considered entertainment a necessity.

Do you like it? her father asked her at the strip mall. And as she sat in the car, reliving the past, she absentmindedly nodded.

"Sofia," her mom said. But Sofia didn't answer. Instead, she remained stuck in her dream world—the place where she lived most of the time. A setting where she could talk to her father and drown out the sound of her mom's screams. "Sofia!" Her mom's words snapped her out of her thoughts.

Sofia opened her eyes and stared at her mom, gritting her teeth. "What is it?" A short, dog-like growl escaped her throat, and she took her feet off the dashboard. With her hand supporting her chin, she looked out the window. Much to her dismay, seeing her mother's faint reflection ruined everything. Sofia hated how similar they looked; her mom's rounded cheeks, chapped pink lips, and dark brown eyes made Sofia a spitting image of her.

"I just want to say, I like what you did to your hair. I never knew cutting it short would suit you so well. That silky brown look is so cute!" her mom squealed while giving a wide smile. But her reflection was enough to tell Sofia it was a forced gesture. Shortly after her mother's compliment, the car went quiet again. She wouldn't let any of her mom's words lower her guard. Letting her in would do more damage to what she had left of herself.

"Nothing will change the fact you divorced Dad," Sofia grumbled. She leaned back in her chair, folding her arms across her chest in the process. For a moment, time rewound. She saw her father standing at his car, a frown embedded into his face, and his confident voice turning into a whisper as he said 'goodbye.' Her mother was merely a demon that birthed her.

"I'm sorry, but we've been through this before. You can't keep talking to me like that." Her mom sighed. At the start of their family therapy sessions, she always chalked Sofia's attitude up to teenage rebellion. But Sofia never believed that. Her mom had to have known initiating the divorce took its toll on her. Of course, she would've been too ignorant to know.

She did her best to look past her mother's reflection and keep her eyes on the road. Staring out of the window, with the snow thickening, it only brought back more memories. She recalled building snowmen with her dad. A small smile spread across her face when the sight of their yard turning into a crowd of snowmen entered her mind.

She called it a 'mosh pit' while her dad called them 'sentries.'

"What do you want for your birthday?" her mom asked.

Sofia turned her head, confused. "What?" Dates and numbers rushed through her head like a flowing river. She'd been losing track of time. Everything from birthdays to holidays never popped up anymore. She felt like a calendar with missing pages.

"Your birthday! It's almost your birthday!"

Sofia scratched her head. For a moment, she considered her mother was just messing with her. "Damn, you're right," Sofia muttered. She'd never met a single person who forgot their own birthday except her father. Although rare, it still happened.

"Did you really forget?" her mom asked.

Sofia took a moment to gather herself. "I guess I did."

Her mom gave a quick nod. "Well, then, it's good I reminded you!" She chuckled. A rare sight that started to become more common since the divorce.

"How about we get some meals at your favorite sushi bar downtown? Wouldn't that be fun?" She slowed down the car. The rumbling of the train tracks they drove over, filled the tension that never left.

"Maybe." Sofia looked down at her hands. Tiny droplets shimmered on her skin. She clenched and unclenched her fist. *Why am I so scared all of a sudden?* "Or you could just get back with Dad."

Her mother's face fell. "I'm sorry. I know you want to spend more time with him, but—"

"Yeah, I know. I still need your permission. You want me to build good habits. You want me to take some time to focus on school, work, and all that other stuff that doesn't mean anything to me."

Her mother sighed. "You can still see your father in your free time. You spent the whole weekend with him last week."

Sofia pursed her lips. "That's not enough. Visiting him every weekend and on a few holidays only makes me wish I had more time with him, and I bet you're keeping me all to yourself on my birthday." Spending another birthday without him wouldn't sit well with Sofia. Her mom's hand tightened around the steering wheel.

"Sofia, just let it go. Our divorce had nothing to do with you."

"Oh, but it did have something to do with you!" Sofia smacked her hand against the assist grip above the door and squeezed it. "I might not be the reason you two split up, but you're the one who started it!"

The frown on her mom's face lingered in her peripheral vision. "I'm sorry, but things just happen. Some parents stay together. Some don't. It doesn't mean we love you any less." She loosened her grip on the wheel. The white around her knuckles faded away as she calmed down. "At least Dr. Hoffman is willing to let us talk together. In fact, your dad has even shown up to a couple of your therapy sessions!" Her mom raised the pitch of her voice. A façade to make her seem cheerier.

"Therapy's a joke. Dad doesn't feel comfortable saying anything around you, and whenever I go alone, Dr. Hoffman just tells me to breathe consciously, and then he talks to me like I'm a kid in every session!" Sofia slumped in her seat.

"Well, I've learned that good things will come out of it eventually. When I was your age, I saw a therapist too. There's nothing wrong with seeing one."

Sofia shot her a glare. "Going to therapy is like being doused in gasoline and having someone drop a match at your feet. It's just humiliating." She took a deep breath. Having to see a doctor for her mental health while her schoolmates were having fun only upset her even more. Even though she didn't have friends at school, she still made sure to have plenty of time daydreaming about making one.

"I know you don't like therapy, but give it some more time."

"I've given it enough tries. It's been months since we started."

Her mom released her foot from the gas pedal. The wipers could barely keep up with the snow battering down, and the darkness didn't do much for visibility either.

"Sofia, please. This will be good for you," her mom said.

"No, it won't." Sofia picked at her fingernails. Ever since her sessions with Dr. Hoffman started, she slowly ground those things down. Her mom looked at her. But just as soon as she opened her mouth, she stopped.

"I understand where you're coming from." Sofia rolled her eyes. Every time she heard phrases like that, she would press her hands against her ears, but over time, her mom caught on. She couldn't avoid her lectures anymore. "No, trust me, I do. My parents got divorced when I was about your age. I also saw my dad as this fun parent. A parent who couldn't do any wrong. But now, I realize that life isn't just about 'fun.' It's also about—"

"Responsibility, I know. I get it. But Dad was responsible. Unlike you, he took the time to be around me, rather than constantly scolding me for mistakes." Sofia shut her eyes again, unable to ignore the beating of her heart. Even short arguments would turn it into a snare drum blasting out notes. To her, the only useful thing Dr. Hoffman taught her was to embrace her anxiety. To admit her fear in the present moment. *The more you resist, the more it persists.*

"We can just discuss the rest of this in therapy."

Sofia took a deep breath, but her pounding heart started to overwhelm her—as if someone was striking a giant stick against its surface, trying to break through. She opened her eyes, leaned forward, and turned up the radio. In her head, she sang along to the music, trying to drown out the rest of the world.

"Please, turn that off," her mom pleaded. But rather than listening, Sofia pretended not to hear her. She nodded until her mom cut off the radio. "You know I don't like it when you blast music." As usual, her demeanor swiftly shifted from caring to annoyance. Sofia saw her face turning red. She swore her mother resembled a tomato almost every time they talked to each other.

"I don't want to go to therapy anymore." Sofia turned her head to the window, fearing her mother's gaze. But this time, she didn't catch it.

"Sofia, you have to keep going," her mom said.

Sofia wrapped her hand around the assist grip above the door. She came to know it as the panic handle. A small device that could make each car ride more bearable. "No," she muttered—a simple word that brought on so many strong emotions. From conviction to anger, it was all there.

"But all this stress has been hard on you! My God, even your father is worried! You say he's scared to speak around me, but he doesn't hesitate to tell me about all your crying sessions!"

"I said, no!" This time, she raised her voice. Her arms shook uncontrollably. Everything she did that was an imitation of her mother made her want to slap herself. So, she took another deep breath. *Acknowledge the anxiety. Acknowledge the fear.* She turned her attention to the road while her mother tapped her fingernails on the steering wheel.

Sofia leaned her head against the window again. The cold air outside accumulated enough to fog up the glass. She drew a heart. After which, she gradually lowered her finger. For the first time, a genuine smile dawned on her mother's face. Sofia saw it out of the corner of her eye. Even though they had their problems, she couldn't deny that the rare moments when her mom smiled at her brought on just as much joy as the times she'd spent with her dad.

"I remember you always loved drawing hearts," her mom said.

A fleeting smile grew on Sofia's face. But still, hearing her mother's voice brought on pain. Even her best moments brought on bad memories.

"Yeah. I also drew them for Dad every day, but now it's just a handful of times every month." Her words seemed to cut deep into her mother's heart. The woman's eyes dropped down along with her lips.

"I'm sorry. But your dad and I had our differences. We just kept fighting. But one of the few agreements we had was to make sure you wouldn't be exposed to that."

"Well, you didn't do a good job with that," Sofia said. "I remember every single fight. I remember how you were always the first to yell. And how you were the first to scream." She hoped she'd left her mother with a sense of guilt.

"You're right. I did, but those were only a few arguments. We kept most of them to ourselves and talked like adults. I chose stances that I believed were for your own good," she muttered.

Sofia closed her eyes again. She gently tapped her index finger against her thumb, hoping the act would let her escape into her memories. Seeing as how her dad would always tease her by tapping her hand instead of holding it, she sought solace in the past. But that hope was soon shattered when her mother spoke again. Sofia gritted her teeth. Sometimes, she almost thought her mother was telling the truth.

The sad tone of her voice seemed so genuine. But Sofia didn't want to accept it. She couldn't.

"Your dad wasn't always right either," her mom said.

At that proclamation, Sofia found the motivation to talk back. "You're wrong." Even the slightest traces of negativity that cast her dad in a less favorable light unsettled her. She didn't want anyone to ruin her image of him.

"Why are you so adamant about blaming Dad?" Sofia asked.

"I'm not trying to say that he's the bad guy. I just want you to know that we both played a part in this."

"That's not true. He always took care of me. He always took the time to talk to you, but you were too stubborn to notice!" All Sofia needed to do was deny her mother's claims. *Deny. Deny. Deny.* She pouted and folded her arms across her chest. Again, she tried to suppress her emotions from escalating even further. But when they were ready to burst, she knew spilling them out was the only form of therapy she could accept. She looked at her mother and prepared to slaughter her with words. "Don't talk about Dad like he's nothing! He's a hero! Unlike you! I mean, all I remember about you was how strict you were! You're not the sweet mom everyone else had!" Sofia elbowed the door before slamming her body back against the chair. "I wish Dad were here. I loved him more than I'll ever love you."

Her mom tried so hard to keep her face straight, but the single tear that dripped from her eye told Sofia just how clean her words cut into her mother's heart. Sometimes, seeing her distraught made her happy, but other times, it made her feel like she was just as brutal as her mom was. So, at some point in every argument, she feared that she also became a festering ball of hatred.

"You and I need to have a talk. We—" but before she could finish, Sofia screamed while pointing to the road ahead.

"Look out!" Her finger warned of a woman in a blue dress, standing motionless in the street. She stretched her arms out like she was an angel flying down, or a crazy woman embracing death. And for a moment, the wind blew against the woman, revealing the red irises hidden behind her long, brown hair.

Sofia's mom swerved out of the way while Sofia bit down on her lip. Their car skidded across the snowy road. Their bodies rolled with the vehicle as they flipped over, smacking themselves into a tree. And, at that moment, Sofia only wanted her dad to hold her.

Chapter 2

With a heavy breath escaping his lips, Hue looked in the rear-view mirror. His mom always told him she'd hand down her minivan when he could drive. He'd taken a few lessons in secret during the moments his stepfather, Harry, was acting like a regular person. Of course, the expected date to own a real license would be after he turned seventeen. The current situation forced him to grow up even faster than he already was. Hue sat at the edge of the seat, shoulders hunched forward, eyes darting between the road and the rear-view mirror.

He was still stuck in the past, specifically, about an hour ago. For the first time, he struck back at Harry. He shuddered at the image of the final blow he gave, which kept invading his mind. He bit down on his lip.

Hue would always conjure possible phrases to remind his mom how close they used to be. He wanted to ask her, *Mom, why can't we spend a Sunday together? Mom, can we go to the movies?* But as Hue silently repeated those pleas to himself, he shook his head.

"No," he muttered. The dream of being able to talk to her—to have a chance where they could spend time together—shattered. Harry was the catalyst for it, but he couldn't pinpoint the final battle that ended everything. The road ahead of him, felt like it was speaking softly. The yellow dotted lines called out. They wanted him to follow the endless road. All the way from their farm out in Iowa to an unknown route. After he nearly finished off Harry, his mom urged him to seek refuge with his aunt. To live with her for as long as he could. Hue didn't want to travel to West Des Moines. He just wanted to travel to a remote location where he could wallow in his guilt forever.

Hue stepped harder on the gas pedal. The punches he threw and the punches he received made his mind riot in a never-ending cycle of mental violence. The recollections would persist for a few minutes, then stop, only for him to have a relapse. He eased up on the gas pedal and put the car on 'cruise control.' With that, he could finally breathe normally. He let his foot rest on the side as he leaned back in his chair, releasing the tension from his shoulders. His fingers reached over to the CD player.

Seeing a CD player in a car used to make him chuckle.

Every time he took a ride with a friend, all they ever used was the built-in Bluetooth connection. The CD slot seemed like an ancient piece of technology to him. But over time, he learned to appreciate it. After all, going through his mom's old music disc never failed to make him smile. Most of the songs were a hit or miss in terms of his personal taste, but there would always be a few he fell in love with. Knowing that a disc was already inserted, he turned up the dial. At first, nothing but brown noise came out. Hue narrowed his eyes.

Frustrated, he punched the CD slot just like how he would do to the TV remote, but when nothing happened, he sighed. *Just give me something to make this day better.* He pounded the slot a couple more times but to no avail. In the end, he reluctantly accepted the fact that he'd have to suffer through the rest of the ride in silence. So, he turned the dial counterclockwise. At first, he didn't notice that the volume remained at the same level, but once he felt a small amount of resistance from the dial, he stopped.

Even the silence he settled for was being ruined by the consistent brown noise.

"Stop!" He hammered the player in one swift motion with his fist. At impact, a soft voice came through the car's speakers.

"Twin Peaks," a soft feminine voice said.

Hue raised his eyebrow. A cold surge washed over his skin. The temperature in the air around him dropped. Even though he'd frequently experienced a range of weather conditions all year, the change seemed too sudden. Too drastic. He pulled the front of his shirt over his mouth. His breaths made for a momentary sanctuary for his face to heat up. In the meantime, he turned up the heater. And once the warm air started flying through the vents, he waited. Anticipating for the heat to fill the car.

"Find me." The voice from the radio spoke again. This time, with a hiss at the end. "Find me in Twin Peaks, and I will offer you salvation." Hue took the vehicle off 'cruise control' so he could bring it to a complete stop. He parked on the side of the road.

I must be tired. He'd never heard voices before, so exhaustion must be taking its toll on him. After all, having stress beating him down as well as Harry's fist... Hue reclined his chair. He rubbed his hands together before resting them on his stomach.

"You'll be taken to Twin Peaks. Find the tallest towers there, and travel fast." Hue shut his eyes. The woman's voice had grown louder. Not only that, but it sounded coarse as if her throat was made of sandpaper. It didn't even feel like she spoke to him over the radio, but rather the passenger's seat. He began to doubt whether this strange experience had anything to do with exhaustion at all, but he didn't have any other idea what was happening. "Hubert." No one ever called him by his real name, Hubert. To him, everyone called him 'Hue.'

Hue's eyes immediately popped open. He held an intense glare at the radio. The temperature around him dropped even deeper. In a split second, frost seeped into the car, creeping over the chairs until stopping at the tip of his finger. His eyes narrowed on the speakers. "You're in Twin Peaks now. Go to the towers, and do not leave the path I set before you."

The volume abruptly cut off.

She was gone. Snuffed out, like the good life he once had. At first, Hue sat there. He fished Harry's winter coat from beneath the passenger's seat. Ever since the man married his mom, Harry's face became accompanied by every cigarette Hue saw and smelt. He grudgingly put the coat on. But as he sat there shivering, it didn't take long for him to notice that the heater had stopped functioning as well.

"Shit," Hue muttered. He pressed the button to turn on his emergency lights, but even those didn't start. He slammed his head on the wheel. Just when things got bad, they got even worse. Hue reached behind the rear-view mirror. His fingers brushed the SOS button, but he hesitated. He was already on the run for brutally maiming his stepfather, so calling for the authorities didn't seem like the best course of action. Hue whispered another cuss under his breath and unlocked his car door. He pushed on the handle, but what felt like an impenetrable defense met him.

He grunted as whatever held it back gave way. Eventually, as he started to move, his face felt an icy sting, and snow covered the road. He needed to get out. Being able to assess his situation became one of his top priorities. Harry always rambled on about the importance of entering a room quickly, usually with a 'buddy,' then clearing the entry point and other tactics that Hue never took the time to listen to. However, he found that within those lessons Harry gave during his drunken ramblings, he could apply plenty of those to real-life scenarios.

This was one of them. *Assess the danger, enter the area, and clear the way.* It might not have been what his stepfather said word for word, but it was close enough. The freezing air, along with a lack of resources, already told him what the danger was. Now, all he had to do was 'enter' the 'area.' Hue shoved his shoulder against the door, causing him to fall outside. He face-planted into the snow, got up, and looked around him—only to feel more lost than ever.

An entire blizzard had formed in such a short amount of time. So fast, in fact, his car didn't leave tracks in the snow. It was like he had just plopped into some snowy apocalypse. Hue watched his breath as it exited his mouth. *What the hell is going on?* He looked to his side. Through the snowy haze, a dark town loomed in the distance. Hue sighed. He wanted nothing more than to avoid everyone at all costs, but fate seemed to force him to play a bad hand. He swallowed his fear and marched toward the town for help. And as he approached, he saw two giant towers.

Chapter 3

Sofia's sense of hearing was the first to return. Even with her eyes closed, she knew the damage must've looked bad. Something dripped. Dripped. Dripped. Next, her sense of touch returned. The next droplet ran from her forehead up to her hair, until it splashed on some surface. Blood, she realized. The injury must be just below her hairline, going down in a straight line. Judging by the aching feeling and strain on her head, she guessed her body was hanging upside-down. And from the moment she opened her eyes, that deduction was proven to be true.

She unbuckled her seatbelt. Her head slammed against the ceiling of the car. Small bits of glass stung her scalp, and with a groan, she crawled out of the vehicle into the thickest blizzard she had ever seen.

"Mom!" she yelled.

However, upon further inspection of her surroundings, she found herself alone. Only the freezing temperatures and the massive layer of snow accompanied her. She knew that staying in the same place was the perfect way to find herself in a snowy grave. The blizzard battered down the vehicle, sending gunshot-like sounds into her ears. And as she stood, shivering, the unfamiliar world only made her heart pound quicker.

Sofia brushed off the tiny shards of glass as she trudged through the snow. The layers of snow soaked her to her knees. Even though she was a short girl at a height of five feet and five inches, a layer this high was too much. Her shoes turned into a tiny swimming pool for her toes.

"Mom!" she called out again. But still, she didn't receive a response. Fear settled in. Her heart felt like it was falling apart. Even though she didn't enjoy her mom's company that much, she'd still rather be with someone she hated than be all alone. Plus, tearing her to pieces in an argument didn't give Sofia that much closure. Even with a preference for her father, she wanted someone to take care of her.

After accepting her fate as a loner, she checked her body. Her fingers ran across her pants, feeling for any tears or holes. All her clothes seemed to be intact, but she felt blood when patting her face, lips, and hands. Cuts from the crash littered those areas of her body. Her once clean face felt like a cutting board, and her delicate hands were rougher. But the cut just below her hairline was the biggest injury of them all. At least for now, the bleeding stopped. She walked around in circles, hoping to catch sight of another person, or even a recognizable landmark. As it became clear that only a winter land awaited her, she let out a deep grunt.

"Mom! Please!" Her throat tightened as she let her voice out. "God dammit," she muttered. With numb hands, she felt her pocket for her phone. Her face warmed up when she retrieved the device. But once she inspected the screen, she saw the dreaded 'x' over the tiny phone icon at the top right corner. *No signal.* She lowered her head. An image of someone giving her the middle finger would've meant the same thing.

Before she could sulk, she caught something moving behind the trees.

"Who's there?" she asked. At first, her chest rose in the hope that it was another person, but once she noticed four furry legs stalking her, her heart turned into a loud snare drum. She backed toward her car. This couldn't be happening. *Four legs. Four furry legs. A wolf? A wolf!* She remembered that as a child, she was told never to run away from dogs since it'd just encourage them to pursue a chase, but would the same apply to wolves? She didn't know better than to assume so.

But before she could get to her vehicle, the animal's hazel eyes gradually shone through the darkness. The odd interaction had a paranormal aura to it. Never before had Sofia witnessed glowing eyes, but she didn't dare to wait around to find out why. Her feet started moving faster. That was when the animal emerged from the darkness. Only then did she stop, let out a sigh, and slumped her shoulders in relief.

Instead of a wolf, a husky dog came out to greet her. And the animal's smiling face and wagging tail only comforted her even more. The dog proceeded to trod toward her. Even though running into another human being would be preferred, she'd still be grateful to have a friendly companion. The animal licked her hand before she held onto his collar. She inspected it closely. The name 'Charlie' was embedded into the metal name tag.

"Charlie?"

The dog licked her again in response. He turned around as soon as she loosened her grip. He howled to the moon before walking toward the trees.

"You want me to follow you?" Following a stray dog in a blizzard gave her a good chance of dying, but staying where she was would just guarantee her death. Nevertheless, a strikingly small chance at survival was better than none. The dog gave her a long stare. They made eye contact one more time, only for Charlie to break it off by continuing his walk. Sofia stood up uneasily. She trailed him through the forest. Twigs snapped under her feet as bullets of snow shot down from above.

The hard trek through the blizzard rewarded her with the sight of a small town in the distance. She stood on top of a hill overlooking it. Two giant towers stood side by side at the other end of the area. Sofia found it odd that such a large structure would be at the edge of a tiny town, but she couldn't waste any more time by asking questions. Charlie sat at the edge, peering down. Sofia nodded. In that instance, they both made the unspoken agreement to head into the residential area that was closest to them. But before they began their journey, Charlie pointed his snout at a wooden sign. It stuck out of the ground. Its words were barely visible in the blizzard. But just as Sofia was about to shrug it off, Charlie ran toward it and scratched the wood.

His paw shook it just enough for the snow to fall off. *Twin Peaks*. Sofia read the name in her head. She had never heard of that town before. She'd been all over Washington state, and she never heard the town mentioned at least once. Then, suddenly, before she could ponder over the town some more, Charlie sprinted down the hill.

"Hey! Wait!" Sofia ran as well. Instinctively, she swung her arms around as she tried to maintain her balance. She couldn't keep up, but the fear of being alone fueled her enough to get down the hill and arrive at the edge of town.

Chapter 4

Hue wondered if he really saw someone running down a massive hill in the distance, but that was the least of his worries. Even if someone really was crazy enough to run around during a blizzard, finding help as soon as possible was what he needed. He marched through the snow toward a dive bar. Its neon red sign lit up the side of the building. Trash bins and garbage bags were just barely visible beneath the snow. Judging by the crushing noise under his feet, the snow hid more items. The more he walked, the harder he breathed.

Each puff of air escaping his mouth turned into fog that quickly dispersed. By the time he stood in front of the door to the building, he noticed a pair of black gloves lying on top of the trash. He snatched them up without a second thought. Much to his amazement, they were just the right size for his hands. The gloves were slightly smaller than that of the average man. A smile formed on Hue's face, once he felt the fabric covering his skin. He let out a deep breath. *Let's go.*

He stepped into the bar, but only received the echo of his footsteps in return. The entire place had electricity, but not a single person.

What the hell? He couldn't come up with any plausible reasons for why the building could be vacant. The lights were turned on, drinks were laid out on the bar, and the jukebox seemed fully operational. Hue sighed. At the very least, the place felt like a sauna compared to the rest of the town. He sat on one of the bar stools to rest. He placed his elbow on the table with his hand raised just high enough for him to rest his head. His chin comfortably lying in his palm.

But his inner thoughts were nothing but chaos. *I'm lost. I just destroyed my mom's life, and now I'm lost.* The memory of his fight with Harry resurfaced. Even though his eyes were fixated on the drinks behind the bar, he saw Harry again. The recollection of sinking his right foot into Harry's stomach felt so real again. The sound of his body shooting backward rang in his ears again, and the sight of his mom crying kept him busy. Up until now, Hue had been able to suppress his emotions. But the mental violence that raged within him took its toll.

Hue slapped the table. His hand turned red, and he cried. Not from the physical pain, but from the memories that wouldn't leave him. *Quick. Make it quick.* Hue told himself to keep his crying session just as short as Harry's temper. He allowed himself a few more hard sobs before standing. He pushed the stool closer to the bar just as he would do with chairs in his mother's dining room. *Guess I'll wait until morning.* Hue's eyes scanned the room for a comfortable place to lay down. One of the booths by the window seemed nice, but the sound of a young boy crying caught his attention. The snowfall muffled his weeping. Hue stormed out of the building, leaving behind a messy trail of snow that stuck to his boots.

Once outside, he shoved his hands into his pockets. He listened intently for another cry but heard nothing. All the houses and apartments had their lights shut off. But then again, maybe someone was still there. Hue buried his chin and mouth into his jacket. He must look like a groundhog with only the upper half of his face sticking out. He placed one foot in front of him but halted when a streetlamp down the road lit up. The orange light appeared suddenly, along with the figure beneath it.

"Hello?" Hue said. Despite raising the volume of his voice as loud as he could, the person didn't react. Instead, they watched him from a distance. "Hey!" Hue slowly approached. As he grew closer, the figure got smaller—it was a child. A little boy. A boy with black hair, just like him. He also seemed to wear the same boots with the same design. The only difference is the size. Even the gloves on the boy's hands were black as well.

Just before Hue could reach the light, it shut off, leaving him in complete darkness. When it turned back on, the kid was gone. *What the hell?* He shook his head. Hue turned his attention down the road to his right before looking down to the left. For a moment, he stopped. Earlier, his hands were shaking, but now, he had finally regained control. *Where did that boy go?* Initially, Hue feared the idea of getting lost in the frozen town, searching for some lost child. But as he remained as steady as a statue, his ears stayed open.

Wind surged past him, and even though the cold stung his skin, that didn't distract him from staying in a monk-like state. For the first time since his hasty car ride, his mind had become clear. He always wondered how he could go from one state of mind to another. Yet, here he was, doing it all over again. As his vision became blurred by the white bullets raining down in front of him, the distinct sound of childish laughter rose from the silence. He looked down the road to his right.

Without a minute to waste, he stomped in that direction. He only wished that the snow didn't cover his ankles. He'd be able to burst into a full sprint otherwise. But as time went by, he reached a fork in the road. All roads at the four-way stop led to completely different areas. It may have been a little hard to see, but he knew that one of the roads would take him to even more buildings, including the two towers.

While another route showed more of a residential neighborhood, he knew ignoring the woman's orders to go to the towers meant he'd remain lost, but he feared that going straight for the buildings would mean leaving the boy to fend for himself.

"Damn it," Hue whispered.

And so, Hue let out a deep breath, and just as soon as it flew through the icy air, he took the long trek toward the neighborhood. As he went on his way, the voice of his mother rang in his head: *I love you.*

He shook his head. The sound felt eerily real, her voice lingering over his shoulder and gently caressing his ears. He could almost feel her arms wrap around him, even. He'd be happy to welcome her back. If only she hadn't neglected him in favor of Harry—the stepfather from Hell.

Chapter 5

S ofia fell flat on her face. Some of the snow slid down her shirt, but at least the frozen landscape numbed her pain. When she got back on her feet, she ran her fingers across her forehead. She didn't feel anything. She wrapped her hands around her upper arms, hugging herself. Even though she went out of her way to get a thick coat before driving with her mom, it couldn't keep out the cold from a harsh winter. With chattering teeth, she scanned Charlie, who sat close to her. His fur seemed so warm it might even make her sweat at this temperature. Huskies were notorious for shedding vast amounts of fur, and right now, she wished she could use the leftovers as a windbreaker.

Her lungs froze with every breath, but she knew the importance of pushing through the pain. She needed a place to stay. Although her heart yearned to see her mother again, she wouldn't be able to fulfill her wish if she found herself lying dead on the ground. So, she took note of her surroundings. Charlie still stood about a foot or two in front of her with his fur ruffling with the strong winds. Judging by the number of stores, she figured they had to have been in the downtown area. Or at least what one could consider as 'downtown' for such a small town.

The only noticeable things were the huge two-story buildings that shot for the sky. If someone were looking at it from a distance, they'd without a doubt believe it to be some sort of sprawling city. Nevertheless, Sofia still felt grateful for having such a tiny area standing before her. A smaller town meant a smaller area for her to cover. As she walked through the streets, lumps of snow fell from the buildings. She couldn't even differentiate where most of the streets started and ended. Did she stand on the sidewalk, or were her feet walking on the road?

Both questions plagued her. Especially since she couldn't find an answer for either one. She knew time was running short with the blizzard growing thicker by the minute. She marched through the urban fields of white, squeezing her arms against her sides, desperate to contain her body heat. She rubbed her hands together as if the friction would start a fire, but even that failed to keep her warm.

"Hello!" Sofia yelled. Raising her voice causes a pain similar to knives being shoved down her throat. Even Charlie showed his concern with a low whimper. Suddenly, he stopped to sniff the air. Sofia halted as well. "Do you smell something?" She bent and petted his neck just beneath his mouth. Then, without any notice, he ran past her. She lost sight of him as he ran around a building with frozen windows. "Wait!"

She stumbled in his direction. Charlie remained an enigma to her, but she thought he'd at least be loyal enough to wait for her. He seemed so disciplined the moment they met, so much to her relief, he still waited by the building. Sofia fell to her knees. Her chest heaved up and down with each exasperated breath.

"Please... don't... don't leave me like that." If she could yell, she would, but the exhaustion of marching through so many layers of snow just took too much energy out of her. "Charlie," she whispered. Slowly, she stood up. The collar he wore swayed back and forth as his tail wagged side to side. Sofia gave him the side-eye. *Of course, you go back to being obedient. Just after you gave me a heart attack.* He continued to sniff around the area. Digging his nose in garbage piles before tearing them apart. Still, nothing came out of most of it. But just as soon as Sofia was starting to grow frustrated, he came back with an extra sweater.

The black fabric smelled horrible, with leftover food sticking to it. But, in that moment, it looked and felt like a gift from God. After Sofia put it on, she rubbed the top of Charlie's head.

"Thank you," she said. Even that small act was powerful enough to instill her with renewed hope. She turned around and tapped on the glass. "Hello? Is anyone in there?" All the lights of every building were shut off. She'd do anything to find someone. It didn't matter if the attempt seemed hopeless. Anything would be better than sitting in the blizzard, waiting to freeze to death. She walked forward, with Charlie trailing beside her, but no matter how many doors she knocked on or how many times she yelled, none of her attempts bore fruit.

Just as she was about to embrace an ice-cold death, Charlie scratched his paw against her sleeve.

"What?" She looked down at him. Charlie raised his paw again to point toward a building standing all alone on the outskirts of the downtown area. Sofia's eyes drifted from his long nails and back to the building. "A place to stay?"

Charlie answered her by walking in a straight line toward the building. Oddly enough, the walk felt much shorter than Sofia expected. Her vision failed to lock onto the building. Not only was her depth perception falling to the wayside, but to her, the world was contorting itself into a strange new place. It was as if the building itself were drawing nearer while the town diminished in size.

She swore every building seemed alive, putting a sense of unease in her heart. She didn't complain for now. She found a kind, furry companion, as well as a possible shelter for her to use. As long as there was a way inside, there'd be a way to stay alive. Once she stood in front of the building, she looked over her shoulder. The entire downtown area was miles away. She shook her head.

"Something's not right," she said under her breath. As soon as she spoke, Charlie looked over at her. He nodded. At the sound of swinging chains, Sofia looked up. Right there, dangling above her head, was a sign reading, 'Little Lambs Preschool.' She let out a sigh of relief. Not only could this place offer refuge, but it gave off an aura of familiarity as well. The name was reminiscent of the religious pre-schools in her hometown. Charlie jumped over the gate leading to the main entrance. Sofia slowly opened the gate, making the chains creak as they gave way. She rushed to the entrance and squeezed the metal handles of the massive double doors. She pulled with all her might, but that only made the snowflakes scrape deeper into her skin. The building was locked. Her face fell. *No, there has to be another way.*

She passed along the brick wall, her legs brushing beside the radiator peeking out. The warmth made her feel safe. Not only that, but the paintings dotting the wall told a comforting tale. They remained completely devoid of snow as if they were being protected. The images seemed to tell a story, broken up into four large panels. Starting from the top left and ending at the bottom right.

First, it showed a herd of sheep. Every animal wandered in various directions. Not even one of them moved with a purpose. In the next panel, a woman in a blue dress kneeled with her hands pressed against each other. She held a shiny green broach in her hands. Despite bowing her head, Sofia clearly saw the resemblance between the figure and the woman who walked in front of her mother's car. The blue dress, the short brown hair—it was all there. What was going on?

Sofia moved her eyes to the bottom panels. The next part of the story featured the sheep following the woman. They now walked in one direction. Their purpose seemed clear. They were meant to follow the woman no matter where she went.

In the last panel, the story ends with the woman staring right at Sofia while the loyal lambs idolize her. Sofia only focused on the woman's face. It was definitely her. She was the same person who walked across the road, forcing a car crash. Her red irises were the most vibrant they had ever been. Sofia found herself getting lost in her eyes. She would've stared at her for the rest of her life if Charlie hadn't started barking from the right side of the school.

Sofia quickly turned her head in his direction. She walked as fast as she could past the gardens running along the front entrance. She heard the pattering of his paws touching the carpet. Instantly, it drew a smile on her face. Her dry lips cracked with the growing grin. A tiny sliver of blood formed with the little crevice of a cut spawning from the sudden movement of her dry face. Sofia walked to the sound of Charlie and immediately felt relief once she saw an open window. Sofia marched forward until she stopped by the opening. As she looked in, she noticed Charlie standing by a bookshelf as he shook off the snow.

Even though she had skinny arms due to the fact she'd sit in the locker room during gym class, the promise of safety gave her the extra strength she needed to climb through. Her arms wobbled as she pulled herself into the building. She ground her teeth together while her knuckles turned a ghostly white. Eventually, she smacked her face right into the carpet. Despite receiving small friction burns from the rough landing, the stinging sensation felt somewhat pleasant, and the blizzard sounded like a distant storm.

When she brought her face up, she realized just how much she took the thermostat in her house for granted. Charlie sat next to her. She leaned into him, snuggling against his body in the fetal position. Her eyes drifted shut. She could feel her mind drifting away. And when the world turned dark, she heard her father's voice.

I'll come back. The world returned to her. She sat straight up, looking all around the room. His voice sent nervous shivers throughout her body. Just one word from him was all it took to make her yearn for the past. Even Charlie could sense the emotional turmoil she felt.

What's wrong with me?

Chapter 6

Hue couldn't help but shiver as he marched through the snow. By now, the white fields had piled up so high, they covered his knees. His feet froze to the bottom of his shoes as the snow crept in there. Despite the unfortunate circumstances, safety and security seemed so close. He yearned to enter one of the houses—to embrace the warmth, dryness, and shelter. He closed his eyes. Images of couches, a fireplace, and heated blankets invaded his mind. *Safety. Safety and security.* But his dreams were cut short when he remembered the times he spent with his mother in their tiny house.

They, too, had a fireplace. Even a weighted blanket that cost a good amount of his mother's paycheck. That was when the cold seeped in again. The entire memory would've been a nice sentiment if his stepdad hadn't barged in. Those memories drifted off into a forgotten dream. Hue let go of a deep breath. He looked to the sky. *Let this nightmare end.* But as soon as he brought his head back down. The path in front of him had changed. Suddenly, the blizzard grew more chaotic, something Hue didn't think was possible. Yet here he was.

The entire neighborhood he set his eyes on vanished. His entire hope snuffed out like a candle without oxygen.

Hue's head drooped. *What now?* He knew the houses lay directly ahead of him. It couldn't be that hard to find them, could it? Even though his vision failed him, he just needed to walk in a straight line. There's no way he'd miss it. He sucked in a deep breath; the winter air stung his throat. However, with the world suffocating him, he had no option but to endure the pain. He forged ahead, stomping through the snow. Each step became a workout as if he was in the school's gym doing squats. And as he kept his head down to avoid being smacked in the face by the bullets of snow, he left his ears on high alert for any potential threats.

"Hue!" The voice of a young boy reached his ears. Hue shot his head straight up. He rested his eyes on the dark figure in front of him. It looked like a tiny shadow formed into a fully-fledged boy. "Don't you remember?"

"I can help you!" Hue yelled, ignoring the kid's question. "I saw a neighborhood up ahead! We'll find shelter there!" Hue moved as fast as he could against the snow's resistance. He didn't know exactly if it was possible to seek refuge there. So far, everything had been abandoned. The entire place was a ghost town. But letting a child freeze to death was the last thing he wanted. He narrowed his eyes at the kid. *If no one answers the door, I'll just break in.* As he got closer, the child turned from a black silhouette into an actual person.

"Remember how good your life was," the kid said, barely audible. As for the meaning of his words, he couldn't figure it out. Once Hue saw his facial features, he couldn't help but stop. They were only six feet away from each other. To him, the notion of taking the boy to safety washed away. He took a good look at him. With his brown hair, brown eyes, and thin cheeks... Hue couldn't take his eyes off him.

"Who are you?" Hue asked, his voice unsteady. The kid was a spitting image of who he used to be. From the messy hair to the slight hazelnut eyes, Hue felt like he traveled back in time. A time when he was just a kid following his mom. "Who—"

His sentence was cut short. The little boy let out a faint giggle.

"You miss being me, don't you?" And with that, the blizzard caught Hue off guard. Just when he thought it couldn't get any stronger, it wreaked so much havoc that he couldn't even see the child anymore, but after about ten seconds, everything cleared. Even the snow stopped falling, and he was left with a vacant winter land. The kid in front of him had disappeared during the blinding blizzard, just like the neighborhood.

No, there's no such thing as the paranormal. I must be imagining things. Hue returned his focus to the same spot the boy used to stand. *Mom always told me I had an active imagination. She said I was creative. And nothing more.* Hue's breathing turned heavy. It took him a moment to realize it, but when he did, he brought himself back to the present moment. His vision honed in on the field in front of him, but no matter how hard he tried, the neighborhood ahead vanished. Even with the snowstorm coming to a halt, he didn't see anything. *No, there's something terribly wrong with this town. Either that, or there's something wrong with me.* Hue shook his head and turned around. Since the kid vanished, he might as well make his way to the towers. The only problem was that looking for the boy put him at the mercy of the blizzard, and the violent storm threw him into the unknown.

Just do something. He told himself. Hue bit the inside of his cheeks. *Turn around. Just walk in a straight line, and we'll find our way back.* And as he inched forward, he couldn't brush off the gnawing sensation that he was being watched.

He traveled alone, but for some reason, it felt like eyes were watching him. He swore he could feel the presence of another human being standing around, wallowing in their own self-pity. He already knew the feeling. Years of practice led to the art of feeling sorry for himself, but to be surrounded by so much sorrow felt foreign to him. He could handle the normal onset of anxiety. Feeling his heart race only to slow down within an instant was normal to him. He knew what his emotions were capable of. It's just that everyone else's feelings felt like finding the meaning of an abstract painting. He couldn't figure it out.

Twin Peaks. He heard a voice whisper in his ear. *A town that you'll leave. But this town won't leave you.* The cold winds that blew past his dried face didn't faze him. All he could sense were the voices.

You have to confess. He heard another voice say. This time, it was a little more feminine. It wasn't exactly like that of a woman. At least, he thought so. Everything started to become a jumbled-up mess. All his senses were overloaded. He shut his eyes tight.

They're not real. They're not real. He kept telling himself. But just as soon he told that lie, he stopped at the sight of a woman standing before him. Her blue dress flowed in the distance, leaving areas of skin exposed to the cold, yet she seemed unbothered by it. An emerald broach adorned her neck. Her hands dangled by her side. The shiniest, reddest apple Hue had ever seen hung by her waist, held tight by its extremely thin stem with her fingernails. Hue didn't know how the fruit didn't get snatched by the hurling winds.

He couldn't take his eyes off her. Neither could he do so for the fruit. The woman raised her right arm. The apple laid delicately on her palm as if she were offering it to him.

Come, take it. He heard her voice vibrate through his skull. At first, they were at a standstill, until Hue instinctively walked forward. He took each step slowly, like he was savoring the crunching sensation under his feet. The closer he got, the more of her features became visible. Her red irises stabbed through the dark backdrop. *Take it. You need to learn. Learn how to repent.* By the time they were merely ten feet apart, Hue reached out to her. Only the fruit held importance to him. All he wanted was the damn fruit. *Knowledge,* he heard her voice say. She wanted something. He just couldn't figure out what it was.

"What do you ask of me?" Hue asked. The words felt like they were torn out of his throat. He didn't mean to speak at all.

The girl. The one with short blonde hair. Find her. Save her, and you might even save yourself.

He didn't understand her cryptic words. The memories of ghost movies he watched with his mother surfaced. All the ghosts, whether good or evil, always spoke in enigmatic ways. He hated that. Listening to their dialogue never failed to make him grind his teeth.

"Tell me, what do you want?" Hue fell to his knees in front of her. For the first time since Harry beat him, he kneeled before someone. Not only that, but he did so unwillingly. His body felt alien to him. He wanted to fight back. To just stand up and walk away, but no matter how much he tried, that didn't seem possible.

Within time, the woman bent over. With the apple still in hand, she spoke to him. "You're here for a reason. And you know what you did wrong. The girl is here, but she doesn't know what she did wrong." Hue looked up.

When her voice rang in his head, she sounded like someone with a strong sense of authority. Each word of every phrase started loudly and deeply as her sentence gradually crescendoed, but as she stood before him, her words had a hiss to them. He locked eyes with her. This time, his mouth reached out to eat the apple. But just as soon as he stretched his tongue, the woman pulled her hand back. "Not yet," she said, waving her finger. And against his own will, Hue found himself bowing his head. "You must-ss lis-listen to me firs-st." Hue flinched as though venom would escape her mouth. "As I said, you know the sin you committed. But that girl—she doesn't know. Find her. Work with her and do everything I say." Hue ground his teeth together. "Take this fruit. Consider it a gift. All you must do is take one bite. One bite and everything will change."

Hue raised one arm. His fingers twitched as it slowly glided toward the apple, but just before he touched it, he pushed his arm down with his other hand. His fingers wrapped tightly around his right wrist. He didn't know anything about the woman. In fact, he didn't know anything about the town. Everything about her radiated untrustworthiness.

"Why don't you just tell me? Tell me what this place is. Tell me who you are. And tell me what you mean. There's no need to be so cryptic!" Hue yelled out loud, his throat opening wide for all the air to freeze his esophagus.

"Because I want you to understand. Understand what I am about to teach you. After all, telling you doesn't ensure you'll learn. A good teacher makes sure their students understand the subject. And don't they say that experience is the best teacher?" Hue ultimately found enough strength to maintain steady eye contact rather than keeping his head low. He got a good look at her. Those red eyes hid something sinister behind them.

She kept the apple steady in front of him.

"Take of this and eat from it for—"

A sudden surge of strength flowed through him. For a moment, he felt like he had harnessed immense power. He let go of his arm and smacked the fruit away with the back of his hand. The snowy hell surrounding them covered the crimson apple.

"Get that away from me," he muttered. "Harry has tortured me enough." He turned his head to the side and shut his eyes. He didn't know anything about her, but he knew a bad person when he saw one. And just listening to her was a dead give-away as well. Because, just like his stepfather, she failed to give clear demands. Accepting her would be like signing a contract without reading it. "Just leave me alone." And with that, the wind picked up. The blizzard came again. An entire barrage of snow pelted them.

You won't come out of here alive. Her voice spoke inside his head.

Whether or not he made a mistake, he didn't know. He just knew he had to get out. But if there really was someone else out there, he needed to find them too. Hue stood. His legs shook under his weight. He shoved his hands inside his coat and stared stone-faced into the distance. Considering that the boy and neighborhood disappeared after a strong hail of white bullets, he expected the same to happen with the woman. And, of course, she did.

He took a moment to turn his head. The apple barely peeked through the snow. He shook his head in disapproval. He then looked away. A clear path stood before him. It wasn't the neighborhood he'd seen before. He didn't even know how he got there, but a preschool with the sign 'Little Lambs' waited for him. He let out a deep breath.

It's time to find some shelter, he told himself, keeping his mother in the back of his mind.

Chapter 7

Sofia woke to the sound of a heavy fist slamming against the front door. The entire preschool shook along with the vibrations. Without speaking, Sofia groggily stood and walked forward. Despite the sudden onset of the blizzard, everything seemed quiet, and once the beating against the wooden door stopped, she only heard the rhythm of her heart. As she strode past the window, she realized the moon was still high in the sky. *What the hell?* Of course, without a clock or a usable phone, she couldn't tell the time, but she felt fully rested.

Sofia looked down and squeezed her hands into fists. *I have the strength.* An odd gesture, but she always measured her restlessness by squeezing her fist. If she had a strong grip, that meant she wasn't tired. She let out a deep breath. Why couldn't everything just be one massive fever dream? She'd rather wake up in Dr. Hoffman's office. Even a horrible therapy session would dissolve her worries right now, but the outsider's footsteps pulled her out of her thoughts. The sound echoed past the side of the building, and Sofia's eyes darted toward the open window.

Earlier, she longed to find another soul, so why did her fear creep in? She sucked in a deep breath, puffed out her chest, and tip-toed to the open glass. Her toes made long strides forward as Charlie rose from his slumber. The dog took one sniff in the air before jumping on all fours. His sudden burst of adrenaline caught Sofia off guard. She came to an abrupt halt. Charlie parted his lips, showing his massive teeth, each of them with a razor-sharp tip. He growled at the window. Sofia cocked her head to the side.

"What is it?" she asked him. But he didn't falter. His eyes were glued to the windowsill. And for only a few more seconds, Sofia heard a single footstep. "Wait!" She reached out to grab Charlie's collar, but he turned feral. His hind legs launched him through the air, and once he flew out the window, Sofia burst into a full sprint. As soon as she got close to the opening, she grabbed the frame with her fingertips. The harsh weather bit into her digits right away. She squinted, and her teeth rattled against the extreme weather.

She pulled her face close enough to the window to get a good view of the outside world, but no one waited for her. *Charlie. Charlie must've chased him away.* She took some time to breathe. She let her chest rise and fall to the gradual decline of her heart rate. Without Charlie, the loneliness started to sink in again, along with the increase of heart palpitations. It felt like her organs tied themselves into a knot. *Loneliness.* That word stuck with her. For each stage of her life, that word held a different meaning. Now, it described the act of losing someone she relied on. Tears slowly well up in her eyes, but the sight of a woman caught her attention. It took a moment for Sofia to recognize her standing under a streetlamp.

Sofia rubbed her eyes. Last she recalled, she was the only person in town. Yet, there stood a woman under the orange glow of a light bulb. It felt as if the town itself was alive and working against her. The place appeared empty the moment she got there, but now, it was starting to reveal mysterious figures just as soon as she trapped herself in a building. The lamp had a low glow, but as it grew brighter, more of the woman came to light. She wore a blue dress with an emerald broach adorning her neck. It was her. The woman who forced their car crash. The woman from the panels.

"Hey!" Sofia shrieked. Half of her voice consisted of anger, and the other half of desperation, but that hardly mattered. Whether or not the woman took responsibility for her near-death experience, Sofia just needed someone to be by her side. "It's you! The one at the bridge, right?" Sofia waved her arm high above her head, but the mysterious woman remained still. After a few more waves, Sofia gave up. Her hand hung by her side in defeat.

The streetlamp flickered. It went dark for only a few seconds, but it gave ample time for the woman to disappear. *Is there something wrong with me?* At this point, Sofia couldn't even trust her eyes.

First, she ended up at a ghost town with the help of a random husky, and now she's seeing a woman in a blue dress. Sofia sighed. Her skinny arms attempted to pull her body out the window. She bit down hard, making her teeth grind against each other, but just as she pulled her torso high enough to gain some footing, a deep croaking noise crept up on her. She immediately loosened her grip. Her frail back banged against the carpeted floor. Despite the excruciating pain, she still felt grateful not to have fallen outside. Sofia crawled backward. She let her ears pick up on the sound.

For a moment, she couldn't believe it. *Am I hearing things, too?* She didn't have much time to ponder, because the deep growl came closer to the window. She didn't want to wait for whoever stood out there—assuming the creature was human. She sloppily got to her feet and bolted for one of the bookshelves. She stumbled a few times on her way there but managed to duck behind one of the cases. With her body concealed behind the stacks of picture books, she peeked out of the narrow sleets left in between the covers of the novels. Her eyes remained glued to the window frame. Just then, as soon as she held her breath, long, skeletal legs crawled inside. A monster. Sofia wrapped a hand over her mouth to suppress her breathing. *Quiet. Quiet.* She repeated those words to herself as many times as she could.

But holding her breath didn't stop her legs from shaking. And as the scraping of the creature's feet grew closer, Sofia shook even more until she accidentally knocked over one of the adjacent doll houses. She let her breath go. In a split second, the monster broke into a sprint. Its skeletal legs carried it across the room in no time at all, while its thin arms swung beside its fat torso. Fear paralyzed her. She readied herself to embrace death, but the short chuckle from one of the dolls reminded her of the gifts her father generously gave her.

The doll let out three short laughs before the memory prompted Sofia to survive. She stared through the cracks, ready to meet the monster. She only saw its feet from here. They had the same paleness as her own skin. As soon as she got on her knees, the thing stopped right in front of the bookshelf. The creature's sudden actions confused her flight or fight response. The monster stood in front of the shelf, Its breath dangling down just as his saliva did. Oddly enough, the heavy air it let out reeked of baby formula. The scent brought back the memories of her childhood and how she wished her innocence would last longer. He turned his head to the ceiling. Something climbed up from its gut to its throat. She watched a lump form at the base of his neck as it slowly traveled upward.

Only when it reached his cheek did Sofia realize it was the creature's tongue. His head fell as the weight forced him to bend to its will, and with his head facing the floor and drool sliding down his dangling tongue, Sofia froze. She couldn't move. No matter how irrational staying put was, moving was impossible. Then the creature smiled, showing off its razor-sharp teeth, and Sofia felt blood rushing back to her face. The creature smashed its shoulder against the shelf. Sofia dove to the floor as the furniture broke into pieces and hordes of books flew through the air. The monster let out a wail. He opened his mouth, diving down to her stomach, but she threw her leg out, making her heel sink into the monster's chest.

She hastily got to her feet after staggering him. For the first time in a while, she ran like she used to on the track team. Her fight for survival became the added motivator needed to encourage a sprint. This time, instead of pulling herself out of the window, she saw the opening as just a single hurdle she had to jump over. The momentum, combined with her will to live, leaped her body forward. She ducked her head while keeping her legs at waist level. She knew her actions would've made her P.E. coach marvel at the sight. But the landing would've definitely done the opposite.

She face-planted into the snow. If the freezing air wasn't enough to wake her up, the frozen ground did the job, but she stumbled back onto her feet before running away. She looked back to see if Charlie was around, but to no avail, and new layers of snow had covered the pawprints.

Chapter 8

Hue continued forward, using his hand as a visor, although the snow had stopped falling. It became second nature in the few hours he spent at Twin Peaks. He expected snowfall. In fact, he was sure a blizzard could hit any second. For now, he bit the side of his cheek as he pushed the thought away. He kept his fist clenched. Feeling as many physical sensations as he could always ensured his mind would stay within the realms of reality. And right now, he needed it. With the strange woman, the desirable red apple, and the little boy lurking in the dark, keeping his wits was nearly impossible. Yet, somehow, he managed to do so.

At that point, he saw a preschool in the distance. His eyes narrowed in on it. Of course, the distance obstructed his view, but he swore a thin silhouette ran in a straight line toward him. He let out a sigh. *More hallucinations, huh?* He raised his head so he could make out the runner. A thin girl with short hair running down to her shoulders.

Hue braced himself for the following events. *This better not be someone made up.* With that, he trudged forward, hoping he could find help. His only worry was that she might have been just as lost as him.

"Hey!" Hue called out. He waited for her to look at him while praying that she wasn't some sort of ghost to torture him. After everything he'd seen, he wanted nothing more than to find someone in this frozen hell he could trust.

A voice had called out, but Sofia kept her mouth zipped shut. She did so involuntarily. Deep down, she wanted to reply to the boy in the distance, but she couldn't find the words. She could only marvel at the fact she ran into another person. A real, and normal person.

"I need your help!" Just as soon as Sofia spoke, the blizzard started again. The boy leaned his ear forward. She feared that the storm would separate them, but as soon as it picked up speed, he ran toward her. His arms flailed wildly by his sides as if losing her meant death.

"If I help you, will you stay with me?" he yelled as he ran. He grunted and tripped, but he didn't tumble to the ground. He stayed on his feet, and once Sofia's eyes met his, the snow stopped. "Let's help each other." The words came out harshly, and with the amount of stress put on by the weather, Sofia wasn't surprised.

Instead, she stared wide-eyed at him. She didn't expect him to close the distance so quickly. But upon seeing him, her heart started pounding just as hard as when the monster intruded.

"Yes, that'd be best." For a moment, she felt like hugging him. She'd never do that to anyone, but considering how lonely she felt since the car crash, seeing another person seemed like getting the car she always wanted. For now, the world revolves around him. She didn't know his name yet, but just like her father, he came at a time of need.

"Where were you going?" he asked. He stood still, the wind blowing against his hair.

"We have to leave!" Sofia snatched his hand. His eyes bulged out. The sharpness of her voice cut through the air. For now, the small talk would have to wait. She needed to get as far away from the monster as possible without losing him.

"Hold on!" His feet firmly planted themselves into the ground. Seeing as how she was no match for his strength, Sofia fell when she felt the resistance he had on her pull. She fell backward. In only a moment, she found herself using the snow as a pillow for her head. Despite the fragility of it, her light body still sunk a few inches into the ground.

"Just take a moment to calm down," he said, extending his arm down to her. On the surface, he looked calm. His face held a strong stare as still as stone, but his hands shook. It could have been from the cold, but Sofia recognized the intensity of it. She always told Dr. Hoffman that shaking from fear looked different than shaking from hold, especially when it came to hands. Sofia wondered how long he'd be able to keep his composure. Nevertheless, he kept his hand out for her to grab. She hesitated but ultimately took his offer. Then, she felt like a feather being tossed into the air as he effortlessly lifted her body.

She brushed the snow off her once she got up but couldn't resist the urge to glance over her shoulder to see if the monster was anywhere nearby.

"Just take it easy a little, all right," he said. "Don't stress yourself too much." Sofia bit her lip. They were wasting time. Time they could have used to get away.

"Who are you?" she asked, her face scrunching up. The boy let out a weak smile. An expression that threw Sofia off.

Hue finally felt some relief. The fact that she took the time to ask for his name showed that she wasn't in such a hurry anymore.

"I'm Hubert." Hue began to shake her hand but stopped. Why had he said his real name? He only let his mom call him that. Their handshake hung in the air for a few seconds longer. Dangling in between them like a dead animal. When she raised her eyebrow, Hue quickly corrected himself. "Yeah, t-that's my name. But you can just call me Hue." He gave an awkward smile. "I haven't seen anyone since I got here." He sucked in a breath. He couldn't tell her about the woman who confronted him—about her command to find a girl with short blonde hair. In other words, a description that matched the girl in front of him.

"I haven't found anyone either." She let out a deep sigh before pulling her shoulders up and looking to the sky. "But then again, I just got here." Hue watched her chest rise and fall with the rhythm of her breathing.

"Yeah, I just got here too," he muttered. She brought her head down. For the first time, Hue found someone as short as him. Usually, at best, most people were a few inches taller, and at worst, he had to stare straight at the sky. Even the girls in the grades below him beat him in height.

"Hey, where did you come from?" The girl got right to the point. By now, her demeanor had calmed down a bit. Hue didn't catch her scanning their surroundings that often. He remained transfixed on her face. The memories of the woman in blue appeared. He just couldn't get rid of her. And that apple. Was he really right to reject it? "Hue?"

"What?" he asked, painfully aware he sounded like an idiot.

"I said, 'Where did you come from?'" She leaned in closer, the tip of her blonde hair grazing his forehead.

"I was driving toward Des Moines, and then I ended up here." Hue looked over his shoulder. By now, the term 'here' meant more of a snowy hellscape rather than a small town.

"I haven't heard of that place." The girl folded her arms across her chest, slightly tilting herself back.

"Yeah, no one really knows that much about the Midwest." After hearing that, she leaned in, sticking her ear toward his mouth.

"What do you mean, the Midwest?" This time, Hue gave her a weird look. His eyes popped open, and he stared at her as if she were an abstract painting.

"You know, the Midwest? The area between the East Coast and West Coast?" She narrowed her eyes at him. Hue flinched. Everything hit him all at once, like a truck hitting him at full force—from getting lost in the town to meeting that horrid woman.

"All right, hold on. What's your name?" he asked through gritted teeth. "Are you one of those university students who just like to mess with high schoolers?" Rather than answering, she turned her head away and looked at the ground. "Hey, answer me!" He reached out and grabbed her arm, but she pulled back. "Did you hear what I said?"

"Don't touch me!" She gently rubbed her arm as if she was wiping away a heavy amount of grease. "My name's Sofia and I'm pretty confident we're on the West Coast." She looked up at him. Despite taking a strong stance about being on the West Coast, Hue knew she didn't know what to believe.

"And I can confidently say, I'm from Iowa. You know, a state in the Midwest?" Hue's gaze never wavered. He did his best to stare right into her eyes, to not show any hint of fear, but his habit of pushing everything down always ended in a massive breakdown.

"No, no, no. We were in Washington! We were driving, and then some woman walked out in front of us and—"

"You were with someone?" Hue interrupted. "Who were you with?" He stood there with their coats protecting their bodies against the wind.

Sofia held her hands in a tight fist. Suddenly, her mom, her fear, and her loneliness weighed her down. She wanted to kneel beneath the weight of her shortcomings. "I was with my mom. I lost her in the crash."

Hue distanced himself slightly. He didn't know exactly what happened to her, but he'd made painful memories resurface, and that felt like getting stabbed in the back of the head. Sofia said, "A woman in a blue dress walked in front of our car. My. . . my mom swerved out of the way, and then I woke up in an upside-down car by myself." Sofia sniffled as a tiny tear drop left her eye.

Hue took a moment to breathe. Even though, he felt bad for her, all he could think of was the woman in blue. The same one Sofia said she saw.

"That woman, what else did you notice about her?"

Sofia looked at him. "What?"

Hue's brain turned into a jumbled-up mess. He needed to learn more about that woman. He just didn't know how, nor was he certain that Sofia felt comfortable enough to open up to him further.

"Let's talk about this later."

"You're messing with me, right?" Sofia spoke only to his back, giving Hue the opportunity to hide his distraught face.

"I'm not. Let's just leave. I need to get to Des Moines." Hue's voice showed defeat. If the world itself wasn't difficult enough to deal with, then everything just got a whole lot worse. He prayed for an escape. To get to Des Moines, find his aunt, and live in secret. Or at least as secret as he can before getting caught.

"No, you have to be joking!" Sofia gave into her emotions, letting herself have an outburst. All the negative thoughts and emotions fizzled together. "We're in Washington! There's no way you just happened to cross the entire country and wound up here!"

"I don't know what happened, but I'm telling you the truth. I'm from Iowa." Hue looked at her, unblinking. And just like his mom, he noticed even a strong woman like her needed someone to rely on.

Sofia wiped her face with her hand, sniffled her nose, and shoved her hands in her pockets. "This is insane," she said under her breath.

"I know. I know it is." By now, Hue had already accepted his fate as being a lost boy. "I promise, I'm not pulling a prank. Especially at a time like this." A strong barrier wedged itself in between them. With Hue, the silence started to set in; he didn't know where to start the conversation. "We need to find a place to stay."

Sofia nodded. "Yeah, let's go back to the way you came from." She pointed past Hue. He turned his head to look over his shoulder.

"There's nothing out there." Sofia took a glance behind her. "We can't go back the way I came from. Some monster tried to kill me." Hue raised an eyebrow. With the little boy running around, and the voices he heard in the dark, her statement didn't sound too far-fetched. However, that didn't mean he was willing to accept it.

"Then where do you suppose we go?" Hue said, just loud enough for his voice to be heard within the howling winds. And for a while, only the sound of the breeze waited in their vicinity, but a deep croaking came closer. Hue stood at complete attention.

"Do you hear that?" Sofia asked. She tensed up, her fight, flight, or freeze instincts probably kicking in. "Let's go!" Sofia reached out for his wrist, but just like before, he stayed firmly planted.

"Hold on a minute," he muttered. He knew staying there was probably a stupid idea, but he needed to test his hypothesis. During their session of extended silence, he considered that they might have been seeing the town differently, at least when it came to its inhabitants. So far, he hadn't run into any monster, only that creepy woman in blue and the little boy. Were they being tortured by different beings?

"What are you doing?" Sofia started to turn frantic. But unlike her, Hue didn't understand her perspective. His eyes gazed into the darkness. Something dragged their feet toward them. They both heard the scraping of skin against the snow as well as the deep growl gradually closing the distance. "Really? Are you really going to do this?" Sofia looked like she was ready to run. "You're crazy," she muttered. She stood by him, her hand on his shoulder. Hue tried to zone out her voice. If the monster were real, he'd run with her. He just needed to see it for himself. The faint sound of his breathing circled them. "Listen, once you see that thing, we're going to run. And if you're not coming, I'm leaving you."

They both waited. Hue felt his heart thump faster. And the closer the sound drew, the faster his heartbeat. "Hue, remember what I said." Sofia kept her teeth tightly shut. Her words came out as more of a hiss than anything else.

Still, though, Hue acted unfazed. His teeth chattered. But then, when he heard the faint cry of a little boy hidden within the croaking, he changed his mind. *So much for testing my idea.* He thought.

"Fine, let's leave." Hue turned around and ran. Sofia's eyes popped open when he began his sprint, but soon, she followed at the same pace.

Chapter 9

Only the sound of their footsteps filled the air for the next thirty minutes. Their mouths remained shut, keeping a silence between them. Usually, such a long session of silence with another person would've made Sofia feel awkward, but amidst all the bizarre events, such a normal feeling made her feel at peace. But while her mind relaxed, Hue seemed so lost in his. Sofia couldn't help but notice his facial expression contort now and then. And so far, the most exciting thing they came across was a street with some parked cars. At the very least, it reassured them they were still in civilization, and she never thought she'd be so happy to see the familiar yellow dashes on every road. The cars and everything else, including the sidewalk, fell prey to the snow.

"Why are there so many of them without a good set of tires?" Hue asked. And yet again, the confusion set in. Seemingly, everything was a brain puzzle. From being able to tell reality from fiction to mundane everyday things, processing it all proved difficult, as if this were a vivid dream—feeling real, and yet something was off.

But despite their horrible predicament, Sofia felt relieved to know they were back in town. They weren't lost in an unknown field, at least, and that thought maintained her sanity.

"That doesn't matter," she quickly said. Her dismissive tone only forced Hue to look even more lost. When she saw his facial expressions, concern melted itself into her. He looked just as confused as she was the moment she arrived. She couldn't read him exactly, but they had to have been experiencing the same emotions. They came under different circumstances, but their mutual fear held them together.

"I'm sorry about crying," she said. Hue just nodded. Sofia sighed. "Yeah, I mean, everything about this place bothers me, but the fact that I lost my mom in the crash is really what makes this bad for me."

"You must love your mom a lot." Hue tucked his chin into the collar of his coat. He let his breath within the fabric warm his lips.

That simple statement felt like jagged knives being driven through her organs. She held her tongue for now. Going on a rant about how she actually hated her mom would've wasted precious energy she could use.

"That's right," she lied. "That's why I need to find her." Hue kept his head low. "You said you were driving to Des Moines. Were you going there by yourself?"

Hue looked up to the sky. "That's not important right now. What we need to do, is find a safe place to stay."

Sofia looked at his eyes.

Hue did his best not to cry, but he failed to stop a tiny bit of water from surfacing. Perhaps talking about her mom again wasn't a good idea. Hue was keen on learning more at first, but now that they'd let their guard down, fear wouldn't be there to shield who they really were. They walked a little further until they came across a statue. Hue stiffened up at the sight. They both looked up.

It was that woman. The sculptor definitely showed every little detail. From the way her dress flowed to the wrinkles on her forehead.

"Hey, let's keep moving." Hue nudged Sofia in the side when he caught her staring longer than he did. Right there, in front of the statue, stood a map etched into a stone slab. His finger traced every road that led up to a hill. "We're right here." He pointed at the red circle in the middle of the guide. He then ran his fingers over the same road he traced earlier. "Up that hill in front of us is the community library. We should take shelter there. It's more than big enough for the two of us. Plus, I doubt we'll find anyone who can tell us about this place. Surely, they have an archive we can sort through. Then we can figure out what to do tomorrow."

Sofia frowned. She already spent a good amount of time sleeping in the preschool, at least she thought, but the morning hadn't come when she woke. Sofia took out her phone to take a picture of the slab, but the red icon for the battery made her hesitate.

Hue looked over. "Are you going to take a picture of it?"

Sofia shook her head. "My battering is running low. If I take a picture of this thing, it wouldn't last. My phone would be long dead. It'd be best if we save this battery for later."

Hue nodded. "That's okay. I'll just have to remember." He took a long stare at the map before beckoning for her to follow him. They marched up the hill.

Sofia would look behind them for any monsters from time to time, but much to her relief, the only footprints there were their own. At least now she could hike up the hill without the fear of being killed. However, with the amount of snow, they had to slow down almost to a snail's pace. The blizzard started to pick up again. Sofia used her hand to shield her face while Hue grabbed onto her.

"Hey, what are you—"

"I don't want us to lose each other," Hue interjected. She wasn't too happy with his actions, to be grabbed without warning. But still, the blizzard always brought something bad. It acted as a curveball, and she understood Hue didn't want to get caught off guard by himself.

Sofia's eyebrows gravitated toward each other as her discomfort made her face tighten. Grabbing his wrist earlier was justified since the impending doom of a monster closing in on them should trump social norms. Yet, she couldn't help but notice how calm Hue looked. Sure, their encounter didn't exactly align with what one might think as a pleasant encounter, but for him to change so fast was hard for her to believe. And with his hand squeezing hers in a death grip, her mind only thought about the inner hatred she harbored. First, she lost her dad, and now her mom. But at the very least, Hue was here when no one else was.

***

The blizzard barely impacted him on the outside. Hue remained stoned face. Every part of him except for his hand was tensed, but as the world became clear again, he finally let go of her.

"What's wrong?" he asked. Sofia retreated her hand back to her side. He realized from her disgusted look that his touch must have bothered her.

"It's nothing," she said.

Hue gave her a side-eye before continuing. Afterward, he gave glances over his shoulder. He bit his lower lip. His fingers pinched the inside of his pockets, and he lowered his head. Every time he stood in the presence of someone so driven by emotion, Harry came to mind.

Not only was the man motivated by his own rage and lust for Hue's mother, but the time he spent with him, only drove out Hue's ability to be himself. He scoffed. Hue could tell Sofia was the type of person who was easily overwhelmed by grief. Most people would rather be partnered with someone who can keep a cool head, but Hue didn't mind seeing a hint of emotion. It made him feel a little more human.

***

Their long and arduous journey finally came to an end. Sofia looked down the hill they had just conquered. Her gratification was long delayed, but even a second of it was worth all the work. She wondered where Charlie was.

"Hey! Sofia!" Hue yelled. She didn't notice him sneaking off to the front door. The library stood before them as a massive gray building—the kind of blandness that made childhood dreams die. Hue tried pulling the handle of the window up. "It won't open." Next, he walked over to the set of doors and tried pushing and pulling on them. "The doors are locked too." Hue rested his head on the door. The inside looked like a warm, haven.

In the meantime, Sofia scanned the entire entryway from left to right. Her eyes took in every little detail she could find. The doors were clean. No damage at all. Not only that but the windows were shut tight as well. Her eyes continued to look over the entrance like the scanner at her school's library.

"How about that?" Sofia asked. She pointed to the vent slightly ajar. Just the top right corner was loose, but she knew she and Hue could force it open together.

"If that's our only way, then I guess we have to deal with it," he said.

Sofia jogged toward the vent. This time, she beckoned Hue to follow her. She got her slender fingers behind the metal and heaved her shoulders back. Her torso wiggled as she pulled the sheet as far as she could. "Help me." She gasped in between grunts.

Hue raised his foot and brought his heel down like an axe. His boot slammed the metal piece farther away from its screws, but after repeated smashes, he gave up. They breathed heavily. Hue glanced at Sofia.

"Well, you are smaller," he muttered. He rolled his eyes toward the shaft. In turn, Sofia sighed. "Let's just get this done." Hue pulled the vent as far back as he could. About two of the screws popped off. "Hurry."

Sofia took off her jacket, gloves, and shoes. Even though she was still fully clothed in her jeans, shirt, and socks, the cold made her feel like she just stripped naked. Nevertheless, letting go of those articles of clothing was necessary for her to fit through the small gap.

"I'll unlock the door from the inside." Hue nodded with a vein popping out the side of his face. Sofia slid in as fast as she could. She crawled forward, feeling every inch of the frozen metal on her bare forearms. Despite the inside being completely dark, the fact that there were no forks made navigation a breeze. She army crawled in a straight path. The entire shaft shook as she moved. And the further she went, the narrower it became. For once in her life, she felt fine with the fact that she weighed a little less than she should have.

Much to her surprise, the other end greeted her like a bright light at the end of a tunnel. Nothing covered the other side of the vent. She quickly crawled out. The feeling of falling on brick never felt so much like a mattress. Not only that, but she finally had more air to breathe. Sofia lifted her head. Her mission objective came back to her.

She just needed to unlock the front door, and they'd be good to go. Sofia speed-walked to the lock and twisted it. Hue stood at the front entrance, holding her jacket and shoes. Upon entering, he handed over her belongings. She watched him enter the main area, her eyes following him like a drone.

"Couldn't even wait for me," she muttered to herself. Her fingers fumbled with her shoelaces, after which she gave up. Instead, she opted to zip up her coat and follow Hue with her untied laces.

Hue was already making himself comfortable on one of the couches. Around him stood shelves of children's books. He lay down on his back, allowing the cushion to accept his aching body. Then, with the small carpet pulled over him, he smiled.

He had an expression on his face that seemed to say, *This must be what heaven feels like*.

Sofia shook her head. Hue didn't come off exactly as the responsible type. But she replayed in her mind how he quickly took the lead. He should be given the benefit of the doubt. She didn't know enough about him to make any conclusions. Her phone vibrated against her leg. Sofia immediately reached into her pocket. The mobile had 'Mom' clearly displayed in the notifications tab. Never before had she been so happy to receive a call from her mother. Eager to hear her voice, she immediately tapped the icon and listened to the message on speaker.

"Sofia..." Her mother's voice broke up over the voice message. Hue stopped beside her. She hadn't even noticed him staring. "I'm at the hotel... we're all here... blizzard... blue..." Sofia's hand formed a death grip around the phone. The device trembled as if it feared her great might. "807 South East... 10th—" The abrupt beep at the end of each voicemail sounded. Having her mother cut off in the middle of a sentence felt like she just witnessed her own death. She frantically pressed the power button repeatedly, but it didn't turn on.

***

"We'll be okay," Hue said. He didn't exactly seem to believe that statement. To say 'we'll be okay' was a habit his mother instilled in him.

Sofia turned to him with weary eyes. With the sniffling noise and shaking mouth, she looked like a monster.

"I have to find that hotel," she whispered. They kept their eyes locked on each other.

However, Hue couldn't forget one of the words in the voicemail. 'Blue.' Sofia's mom said blue. All he could think of was that blue dress. But just as he opened his mouth to address his concerns, Sofia's voice barged in, "I can't let this slide. Now is my chance." Sofia shoved the phone into her pocket. "Where's the hotel?"

"How am I supposed to know?" Hue held his arms out after shrugging.

"You don't remember the map at all?" she asked.

Hue sighed. "If I had that good of a memory, I would've told you by now! I only focused on where we agreed to go." Hue shook his head. That look she gave him was all he needed to know. Her wide eyes and tightly sealed lips meant that she had a strong motive to take action. "I'm just as lost as you." He tilted his head back to look at the ceiling. He hummed, pretending to be thinking of a solution. But Sofia just rolled her eyes at him.

"Fine. I'll figure it out myself." She placed her hand on his chest and pushed him away. She stormed past him into the old archives of the town. As Hue stared at her dumbfoundedly, she ran her fingers across the first shelf she reached.

***

Sofia started from the newest-looking book, believing that it'd be the most up-to-date and hopefully contain the most recent information the town had to offer. She snatched it from the shelf only to see an image celebrating the town's opening. She brought the book up to her face, flipping through all the pages.

In the end, Sofia concluded that it held no useful information, but upon opening the next book, she saw a little girl. It was merely a pencil drawing but detailed enough to feel like a real picture. The child stared back at her from the page. She wore a long dress that flowed down to her ankles and a broach almost as tall as her neck loosely hung to her. Above the drawing was written in elegant handwriting the name 'Dabria.'

Hue looked over, noticing that she had stopped searching for new books. Thinking that she had found a map, he rushed toward her. He told himself that if he saw even a tiny image of a road, he'd tear the book apart. But, when he looked at the little girl, he stopped as well.

"Who are you looking at?" he asked. Sofia pointed to the name written at the top of the page.

"Her name's Dabria. Look." She also pointed to the broach. Hue let out a deep breath. He dug his nails into his hair. That woman had to be the woman in blue or at least have some relation to her. The facial features were somewhat similar, but her wardrobe caught his eye. Sofia placed her finger under the page, but before she could flip it, Hue pleaded with her not to.

"No!" he demanded. Sofia glared at him.

"Why are you against helping me?" Sofia sneered at him.

Hue thought about the woman in blue. Even if what she said about Sofia was just a jumbled salad of words, he still feared going outside. He knew the woman wanted something.

"That kid has to be the woman in blue!" Hue blurted out.

"So?" Sofia rolled her eyes.

"Listen, I saw her earlier. She told me some weird things about repentance and finding you and—"

"Wait?" Sofia said. "We've been traveling together for a little over an hour, and now you're opening up to me about all of this?"

Hue squeezed his lips together. "Yes," he said, defeatedly. "From what she said, I know she wants something to do with us, and I'm scared to find out what it is."

Sofia held the book in front of them. Her hands remained frozen, but just as soon as Hue reached over to shut the covers, she turned her back on him. "Well, we're never going to find my mom by staying in here, and we definitely won't leave this town either." She flipped to the next page. This time, she relaxed her shoulders. "It's a map." She faced him, shoving the book in his face.

A picture of the woman ambushed Hue's eyes. This time, it was a fully colored photo. She smiled at the camera. The broach that the little girl wore fit her perfectly. And at the top of the page, read a small scripture.

I, Dabria, am proud to lead my church. May we help those in need. It was a somewhat generic statement, but seeing as how it was from the woman's own mouth, Hue felt uneasy. The photo even harbored distraught-looking teens just like him and Sofia, as if she were targeting them specifically.

Unlike him, Sofia didn't seem to care. She ignored the picture and tore off the bottom half of the page that held the map.

"Let's go then." Sofia folded it up and put it in her pocket.

"Fine," Hue muttered.

They walked together toward the center of the library. "Hey, Hue?" she asked. She sat on the floor to read the map while Hue sat down on the couch.

"What is it?"

"When my mother said she and everyone else are waiting at the hotel, do you actually believe that?" Sofia kept running her fingers over the roads, showcased by various thin lines running over the page.

"I don't know." Hue sighed. "We haven't seen anyone else besides the woman in the blue dress. This town is probably empty. That voicemail must've been the town messing with us." He looked out the frosty windows at the other end of the room. They stood above the broken heaters behind the bookshelves. He gave a long stare, losing himself at the sight of snow trampling the world. Sofia gave him a side-eye.

In the end, she folded up the torn page. As her hand shoved it into the depths of her pockets, she let out a deep breath, hoping it would catch Hue's attention. And when it didn't, she spoke up.

"Well, I believe it." She kept her answer simple, but to Hue, her words may have more layers than what he heard. He fought back the urge to call her on her bluff. She was definitely putting up a façade. A façade of false confidence.

"Okay," he muttered.

Sofia turned her head toward the front door. Just outside of it waited the lobby. The only buffer zone between them and the exit. "I just want to find my mom first." Sofia held plenty of concern in her voice.

Hue's ears picked it up like a magnet. He could tell by the strain in her throat and the rise in her pitch that her relationship with her mom was just as complicated as his.

"If she's hiding out in the hotel, I'm sure she'll be safe until morning," he said. Sofia opened her mouth, but Hue had already gotten comfortable on the sofa.

"No, I have to—"

"Sofia, I do realize that you want to find her, but do you really think she wants you to risk your life out there in the snow?" By now, Sofia's stance wavered.

"I already told you; I need to get to her!"

Hue shook his head. "Come on, let's just wait it out," he spoke softly. And unlike their previous conversations, he kept the little boy in mind. After all, Hue was a diplomatic child growing up. He extended his arm out, making a circular motion over the floor. "There's a good sleeping spot for you right there," he said. Sofia didn't answer. "I'll let you use the carpet." For about a few seconds, he became a salesman for carpets. He rubbed the fabric, allowing her to hear the friction.

"No thanks," she said disappointedly. "Now that I'm not in the vent anymore, my clothes will keep me warm."

Hue shrugged and rolled over on his right side before closing his eyes, and while Sofia shuffled around to get to the floor, he pretended to sleep.

"Hue." Sofia just couldn't help but pour out her thoughts. And going under the assumption that Hue was sleeping, she felt out of place.

"What is it?" He rolled on his back and kept a steady gaze on the ceiling.

"I'm sorry for acting so reckless," she whispered.

He raised his eyebrows, happy that she couldn't see his face. "What are you talking about?"

Sofia sighed. "Well, I was really frantic when I ran into you. Not only that, but I was ready to drag you outside with me to find my mom." Hue let out a deep breath. His hands trembled on his lap. His fear of the outside surpassed the relief he felt from staying inside. Sofia turned her head.

"Are you cold?" she asked. All her attention went toward his shaking palms.

"Yeah," he lied. Hue tried to close his eyes, but Sofia's presence felt like fingers prying them open. "Actually. . ." They made eye contact, prompting him to keep his mouth shut. He was stuck in an icy hell, but being too scared to tell the truth hurt.

"There's something else bothering you, isn't there?" Sofia stated. His eyes were still on her. "My mom always said one thing but meant something else. I've learned to develop my own lie detector." Hue rubbed his forehead. He racked his brain for possible conclusions.

Does she know why I'm scared? Does she? Or does she only know that I'm scared? Those were the questions that ran through his head. But the harder he bit down on his lip, the more Sofia felt inclined to get to the bottom of his feelings.

"It's that woman."

Sofia slowly sat up. "Are you talking about Dabria?" she asked.

Hue nodded.

"To tell you the truth, I talked to her. I talked to her face to face."

Sofia stared at him. "Was that when she told you about me?" She crawled toward him. "Why don't you tell me everything?" She raised the pitch of her voice, making it even more feminine than it already is.

"I'm just scared. She mentioned you, and she mentioned me. According to her, I'm here for committing sins, and so are you." Once

Sofia sat on her legs in front of him, Hue rotated his body so that they were facing each other.

"What are you talking about?" Sofia asked.

"I'm just telling you what she told me. Apparently, we're bad people who do wrong." Hue wished he could take back what he said. The weight of his words pulled down Sofia, and her reaction spread to him.

"How did I do something wrong? I'm only here because my mom crashed! Not only that, but we'd never have driven on that road if my mom hadn't torn apart my family with her stupid divorce!"

Hue grunted. Sofia wasn't the type of person to do bad things. Her slender frame made her seem more like a broken-down rag doll rather than a fighter. But then again, he's never met a single person who liked to admit they were wrong.

When it came to him, however, Dabria had to have been referring to Harry. There's no one else he hurt. But why should he be punished for fighting back?

"I don't know," he muttered.

Sofia dropped her head. "This place is insane." Her breathing gradually increased.

Sensing her anxiety, Hue sought to comfort her. "I understand what you're going through," he said. Sofia brought her head up to glare at him. "No, trust me, I do." He was hoping she'd just nod her head and feel a little more relaxed when he tried to relate to her, but when she waited for him to elaborate, he found himself weaving his words into an intricately made basket. "My relationship with my mom is strained, and I don't have a dad either." Sofia eyed him. Hue set himself up to be vulnerable.

"Why?" Sofia asked. Hue's eyes opened wider. "Why did your family end up that way?"

"When my real dad left, my mom only had me, but I guess she got lonely. Then she met my stepdad, and that was the end of everything." Sofia nudged him, but he refused to reveal more.

"What else?" Her eyes grew wide. She wanted to hear every semblance someone had to her life. It didn't matter if those similarities were small or big; she wanted someone to relate to her.

"I'll just say, my stepdad isn't a great person, and my real dad wasn't around long enough for me to know if he was good or bad." She tried to ask another question, but Hue rolled over on his side and dismissed her with a wave of his hand.

"My parents got divorced a year ago," Sofia said to his back. Even though he didn't turn around, she knew he could hear her. "I always wanted to live with my dad. It's just been a nightmare living with my mom. I wish he had custody of me." After her brief introduction to her past, she lay on the floor again. Now, she wished she'd taken the offer to use the carpet as a cover. At least then she could hide herself under it. She wished Charlie was here too so she could cuddle away her sorrows. From then on, she shut her eyes, and shut off her brain, while Hue did the same.

Chapter 10

Sofia woke to the sound of a massive snowball slamming against the glass. Her body shot straight up. With her chest rising and falling rapidly, she scanned the room. Hue still slept, slowly breathing in cadence with his heart. Sofia turned her attention to the tall windows. A downpour of rain battered the ground outside. Even though the blizzard had lightened up a tad, that still wasn't enough to indicate a large passage of time. The mental strain from the endless night would just be another obstacle to overcome. She rested her head on the floor and closed her eyes. *Sleep. Sleep.*

But no matter how much she repeated that phrase, nothing would come of it. She rolled over on her side, shifted around, and then rolled again. Eventually, she found herself lying on her back, but even that didn't encourage sleep to take over. Her eyes still resisted the urge to shut.

"Damn." She sighed. Her fingers picked at the carpet, hoping to pass the time. But just as soon as her digits started making their own rhythm, small paws tapped throughout the lobby. *Charlie!* Sofia had almost given up any hope of seeing the dog again. She quickly stood. Hue didn't stir when her quick movements blew the air around her. Sofia trotted toward the lobby. As soon as she exited the doors, she stretched her arms out, ready to greet Charlie, but he kept his back turned to her. His tail hung behind him like a dead snake as he looked out of the window.

"Charlie!" She squealed at him. Her arm stretched out for his forehead, but rather than giving her the chance to pet him, he turned his head and presented her with a piece of paper he held tightly in his mouth. "What's that?" He opened his jaw. The page flopped on the brick floor like a dead fish. Sofia knelt. When she retrieved the paper, she unfolded the thing.

Another drawing of Dabria.

She stood between two men in this picture. They wore dark robes. Both men towered over her. They dawned black gas masks. However, they had an odd design. Instead of having air filters in the front, they had a long tube that extended from the mouth, all the way to a bag strapped to their hip. Just like the other picture, it was a mere drawing, but the detail in its lines, shades, and colors etched itself like a permanent photograph. "What is this?" she asked. Rather than doing anything mystical, he behaved like a regular dog, wagging his tail while breathing heavily with his tongue out.

She let out a grunt before taking another look. The talk she had with Hue resurfaced. *That woman said we've sinned.* Sofia shook her head. This town was definitely off, but she still found it hard to believe she'd have done something horrible enough that warranted a meeting in hell. When she lifted her head, Charlie was nowhere to be seen. She only found the glass doors in front of her. Her heart fell once the realization set in, but she remained steady. Her hands were quick to refold the page and shove it in her pocket along with the map.

Charlie was her only other companion, other than Hue. Those boys kept her sane. However, Hue was like a double-edged sword. He was the only human companion she had, which kept her mind in check, but he was a mystery she had to unravel. She wished he wasn't her only human companion. Sofia let go of her worries for the moment and returned to the reading area. Her legs got heavier as the stress returned to her. The pages in her pockets felt like rocks.

When she came back, Hue was missing. Judging by the fresh imprint left behind, she knew he only left recently.

***

Hue weaved through the bookshelves. Deformed shadows lurked outside. Initially, when he heard them, he noticed that Sofia was gone. It didn't take long to find out that his assumption of Sofia walking about the library was dead wrong. His eyes caught a glimpse of two of the creatures staggering in the snow. Much to his dismay, Sofia was right about the monsters. Not only that, but their awkward shuffling, fat bellies, and frail limbs made them look like toddlers trying to walk. They were also naked with the anatomy of a doll.

"Hue!" Sofia yelled. He popped his head around a bookshelf. "Hey, Hue!" Just like a cat, Hue moved at lightning-fast speed without making a sound. In no time at all, he came within grappling range. While he managed to remain hidden right behind her, he placed his hand over her mouth. Sofia let out a muffled scream, but Hue responded with a soft shush.

"It's only me," he whispered. "I'm going to let you go, but I want you to stay silent." As he slowly released his grasp, a shadow passed through the window.

"Monsters?" she asked, just to make sure. Hue nodded. A pale figure tapped their forehead repeatedly against the glass. Both their faces turned white, but a little bit of color returned when they realized the creature was blind.—the monster had empty eye sockets.

"Be quiet," Hue whispered.

Sofia turned and pointed toward the lobby. "Let's go through there." She kept her finger raised.

Hue shook his head. "While I was looking for you, I found an emergency exit. It seems more discreet to me." He jogged just at the right pace so that his feet were quiet, and he closed the distance quickly. Sofia followed, although a little clumsier. When Hue placed his hand on the door, he stopped. "I'll peek my head out. If it's clear, I'll tell you."

Before she could even acknowledge him, he peeked his head out. The air still felt like dry ice, but the snow finally came to a halt. When he looked up, the sky was devoid of everything, even flakes. "It's clear," he said, bringing his head inside.

Hue held the door open for her, and together, they slipped out of the library unnoticed.

***

With the distance they covered, Sofia and Hue took a moment to breathe. They made sure to hike at least a few blocks away from the library before taking a break.

"Now, what?" he asked. He waited for her with his torso completely bent over. He firmly held his hands on his knees. Even with the low temperature, sweat still found a reason to soak his forehead. Sofia thought back to what Charlie had given her. They had already seen Dabria a few times, but those men, who were they?

"Look at this." Sofia pulled out the drawing.

Hue grazed the page with his fingers as though he could reach into the picture and actually touch them. "Who are they?"

Sofia shrugged. "I don't know, but if they've been hanging around Dabria, let's hope they're not here still." She handed the image over to Hue, who studied it carefully. Meanwhile, Sofia took out the half-torn book page. All she ever used was the GPS on her phone, so it took her a while to process a real map.

Once Hue was done, he shoved the paper into his pocket sloppily. As soon as he noticed Sofia pondering over the map, he stepped in. "Let me have a look." They huddled together, each of them keeping their hand on the map. "Here." He firmly stabbed his index finger onto a road. "That's where we are, and over there is where we need to be." He moved his finger along a winding road that existed in a sub-urban neighborhood. The path eventually divulged into a four-way stop, but the hotel was indicated to be down a straight line.

"That's a really long trek," Sofia said. Her legs were already burned from all their walking. She swore that the sight of the monsters affected more than her mental well-being.

"Then that just means we have to start as soon as possible." She folded the map before neatly putting it in her pocket. However, just as soon as Hue took the initiative, she called out to him.

"Wait!"

He stopped in his tracks to face her. "What is it?" His voice had a hint of agitation. Considering that the safety of the library had been compromised, he wanted to find shelter as soon as possible.

"It's just that. . . Dabria, that woman we keep seeing, what do you think makes her so important to this town?" She reached into her pocket once more, but Hue raised his hand to stop her.

"You don't need to show me that drawing again. She's probably just some fanatic in a town full of fanatics." He spoke quickly as if to disregard Sofia.

She felt a stabbing sensation in her heart. The unknown made her uneasy. She knew it bothered Hue, but she wished he would be open to her.

"Where'd you get that drawing? The one with the two men?" Hue asked.

Sofia shrugged. "This dog, Charlie, gave it to me."

Hue eyed her. In the short time they knew each other, he didn't recall her mentioning any animal companion.

"Dog?" he asked.

Sofia shook her head. "It doesn't matter. What matters is that this woman has been following us. She's a statue, she's a drawing, and she's a real person." Hue quickly nodded.

"Yeah, but first, let's just worry about getting inside." He stood with his arms folded across his chest. He waited patiently for her.

"Here." She handed him the map. "You're definitely better at directions than me."

Hue gratefully took it. He proceeded to keep it safe inside the warmth of his coat. From then on, they walked side by side. Moving forward, according to a few roads, they could see. Even though snow buried most of the landscape, neither of them complained. They saved their energy for walking instead.

Eventually, they reached the neighborhood that stood between them and the winding road. It looked just like the residential area Hue saw earlier. He only hoped that it wasn't the same one. If the place were always shifting, then their map would be useless. The houses looked more modern than the ones in his neighborhood.

"This town is really something else," Hue muttered. Sofia flinched. They had been keeping quiet for so long, she felt like he wasn't even there. "The houses back in my neighborhood were a little older. More run down, I guess."

Sofia placed a hand on his shoulder. "Like I said, we're nowhere near your home. This is a completely different state," Sofia said.

Hue nodded. "It's probably a different world, too."

His quick response made Sofia shudder. She didn't want to accept it, but she knew they weren't in an ordinary town. They probably weren't even in the real world.

"As bad as it is, I'm pretty sure we're in hell, or at least someplace that's like hell." Sofia sighed but let him continue. "With these monsters and the never-ending blizzard, don't you think all of this is meant to torture us?" The snow suddenly thickened, obscuring almost all of their vision.

"Let's keep moving," Sofia said sullenly, wanting to forget their dire circumstances. They were being toyed with. The snow soon covered Hue's coat, making him look like a snowman, yet despite that, Sofia still wanted to continue their conversation. Letting him go wasn't part of the plan. However, focusing all their energy on moving forward was obviously something he put at the forefront. He didn't care about small talk as much as she did. In a way, she felt grateful. Her heart still raced at the idea of the monsters roaming the streets.

Not only that but if those supernatural beings didn't take them, then surely the cold would.

"Are you sure about that?" Hue yelled over the wind. "Those things have been walking outside. They don't even have clothes on. The snow doesn't make them flinch!"

Sofia let out a deep breath. "You're right." She didn't want to admit it, but he was. She tried to gauge his hardened expression. Whether or not he was thinking about the creatures or just focused on walking, at that moment, she didn't know.

"Did you also notice how they looked like babies?" he asked out of the blue. Now that he said it, Sofia was reminded how the first one smelled like baby formula. "I haven't thought about it before, but yeah, you're right."

"Do you think they look that way for a reason? Like, maybe the town wants us to see them that way?" Hue asked.

She took in one more breath before picking up the pace. Again, his feet scraped against the snow as he dragged them forward. This time, though, Hue struggled more. The sudden chaos of the blizzard put a wedge in their plans. While the snow had always been thick, the brief time they had without it, spoiled them enough to put their guard down.

"How far are we from the hotel?" Sofia asked.

"We're—" A high-pitched scream boomed around them. They turned their heads simultaneously.

"Do you see that?" Sofia pointed at a feminine figure in the distance.

"Yeah." She noticed Hue's voice shake. His tense hands did the same. Sofia narrowed her eyes on the figure. It slowly walked as if they were gradually freezing in place.

"No. . ." she muttered. That's when Sofia saw it for what it was. When it came within eyesight, she noticed every little feature of the monster. The two-faced being shuffled toward them with its long, ingrown arms hidden beneath its skin. Without speaking, they broke into a sprint, creating as much distance as possible between them and the creature. While Sofia's breath grew heavy, Hue only grunted slightly. The speed at which he ran stirred up a strong sense of jealousy within her. Suddenly, she regretted lying in bed all day. Back then, she cursed the sun for waking her up in the morning. Now, she just wanted it to come out. After sprinting for about a minute, Sofia looked behind her.

"That thing is getting faster!" she spoke in between breaths.

"Just keep running." By now, Hue started to show hints of fatigue. He could barely get the words out of his mouth. Their run became far too vigorous for them to speak like normal people. And again, when she turned her head, the monster was still hot on their heels.

"Oh shit!" Hue's sudden outburst caught her attention. The neighborhood shifted all around them. The houses moved around like blocks being pushed toward different angles. One moment, a house would be in front of them, and then the next, it slowly twisted until it ended up in another spot. Even then, more monsters appeared. Some would show up only to vanish within a few seconds, while a few remained in pursuit. The world blurred and distorted into nothing and everything.

"What the hell is going on?" Sofia heard the wind blow past her ears. They bombarded her cheeks, making her wish she could cover up.

"I don't care!" Hue said. "All I care about is getting us out of here." He looked forward, behind, left, then right but couldn't come up with a decision. Nothing made sense. There wasn't a straight path they could follow. Sofia began stumbling as the distortion took effect. Her brain felt foggy, and her head turned dizzy. Bile started to get ready to burst through her lips. "Shit!" Hue yelled. He grabbed one of Sofia's wrists. "Stick together!"

As they ran forward, they saw two monsters sprinting at them like a bull with its horns out. Hue still charged forward, gambling on the idea that the roads would shift again, giving them a chance to escape.

"Look!" Sofia pointed to their right. A road appeared, welcoming them to follow it. Hue wasted no time in changing directions. The copious amount of sweat that formed around her wrist made her slip out of Hue's grasp.

But as he felt her lose contact, she kept telling him to run.

"I'll be right behind you." She panted. The street sign of the road appeared next to them. Hue stomped his foot deep into the snow as he went around it.

"God dammit!" Now, when they looked back, the number of the monsters turned to five. Each one clumsily moved like a child. Hue stood in a fighting stance. To him, running proved fruitless–they'd just get themselves in more trouble as they lost their way. He bent his knees slightly, getting ready to fight for their lives. "Stay behind me," he told Sofia. Without waiting for a response, he acted as her shield. Sofia bit down on her lip. She knew fighting would be suicide.

She turned around, praying that the road would distort again, but instead, her eyes locked onto a house. The lights were still on.

"Hue!" She grabbed his shoulder. He focused on the house she pointed at. The blue residence had purple curtains covering the windows, but the light emanating from behind the fabric cast the shadow of a short girl walking across the room.

"Go!" he commanded. Sofia ran as fast as she could. Hue followed closely. After she mounted the porch, the monsters were almost within ten feet. This time, they broke into a sprint. Hue picked up a flowerpot on the side of the steps. He chucked it at one of the creatures. The clay piece shattered on the monster's head, knocking it down. "Get that damn door open!" Sofia frantically slammed her fist against the door. She tried twisting the knob. However, it didn't give way.

"Hey!" Sofia slammed her hand against the wood one more time. "I know someone's in there! I saw you walk past the window!" She pounded it again to no avail. "Let us in!" A tiny set of fingers slightly pushed the curtain aside. It gave just enough room to let the small head of a child peek through. "I see you!" Sofia yelled. She waved at the little girl, but she popped out of view. "Let us in, please!" By now, one of the monsters stepped foot on the stairs. Hue brought his arms back before throwing it full force at its face. A cracking sound rang in Sofia's ears as it fell back.

"The door!" Hue screamed again.

"Who are you?" the girl asked within the safety of her own home.

"We're just trying to get through the town. There are these things out here trying to kill us." Sofia turned from a squealing, frightened teenager, to someone getting ready to embrace death. She spoke softly to the kid. "Just let us in."

"I have to ask my mom if you can come in!"

Sofia heard her small footsteps recede from the entrance. She guessed that her incessant yelling only made her feel uneasy. The third monster finally reached them, and it stretched its arm out. His limb shot past Hue's face and gripped Sofia's collar. The monster pulled her to the ground, but Hue didn't hesitate to kick it down. After he pulled her up, he mounted the beast, bringing down a flurry of punches to the head. Eventually, it stopped moving, leaving only Hue's cut knuckles in its wake.

"Forget that," he murmured. With all his strength, he picked up the wooden rocking chair in front of the window. Sofia stared at him. The thing looked like it was about as big as him, but that didn't stop Hue from throwing it through the glass. It shattered the window. The piece of furniture broke into bundles of wood when it hit the floor. "Go!" Hue helped Sofia crawl through the window. Her long sleeves protected her arms from the jagged edges, but she still managed to get a small nick on her fingers. Then Hue gripped the frame, ignoring the painfully sharp glass and pushing himself inside.

His face turned red in the process, but once he slammed onto the floor of the house, his skin returned to its normal color. When Sofia took another glance outside, several monsters were skulking toward them. They formed a horde hell-bent on taking their lives.

"Sofia!" Hue's voice pulled her out of her trance. When she looked at him, he was pushing a bookshelf in front of the window. Sofia hastily joined him at his side. Together, they created a blockade to keep the monsters out. Hue moved more furniture toward the window. He took the chairs sitting in front of the fireplace, using them to reinforce their barricade. Through the small crack they left, Sofia saw the world become distorted again. Now, the monsters vanished, relocating to some unknown area. Sofia let out a sigh of relief. Even Hue let his shoulders slump.

"Then that's it, huh?" Sofia asked.

"Yeah, for now." They both took a moment to rest. All that remained was to look around the house and find the girl.

Chapter 11

They took their time snooping around the place. Sofia's eyes left nothing unscanned. Neither the girl nor her mother revealed themselves. The only remnant left behind was a picture of the child, standing on the mantle of the fireplace.

"She's not on the first floor," Hue said, returning from the kitchen. He took deep breaths as he rested his back against the bookshelf.

"I know." Sofia nodded. She opened the closet under the stairs.

Despite seeing the monsters vanish before their very eyes, Hue still made sure that he kept the shelf steady as long as possible. In the meantime, Sofia's journey into the closet bore no fruit. Hue pressed his back harder against the shelf until both of them heard the sound of furniture scratching the wooden floor. Hue turned his head to the top of the stairs.

Sofia took a glance. Now, as he jumped into action again, Hue led the way up the steps. Sofia followed closely behind him.

"Give me some space," Hue whispered.

Sofia went down one step. She was practically holding onto Hue's shoulder, and he knew, if they were attacked, he'd need room to fight. Once they reached the second floor, they walked past two doors, stopping at the room where the sound came from.

Hue stared at the bedroom door, expecting a monster to burst through. He placed his hand on the knob. He silently counted down from three to one. As soon as he lowered all his fingers, he burst into the room. His shoulder slammed through the door. Sofia stumbled in even less gracefully than he did. Standing before them was the horrified face of the little girl clutching the leg of a woman. They huddled in front of a single bed. A pile of items lay on the mattress. The woman had her arm outstretched toward the closest object. In a flash, she chucked a lamp at Hue's face.

He ducked, letting the appliance shatter on the wall behind him.

"Wait!" Sofia yelled. The woman snatched an umbrella. She sprinted toward Sofia, swinging it wildly in the air. Hue grabbed the umbrella and yanked it out of her grasp. She backed up and hugged the little girl, smothering her in her red scrubs.

"Heather, stay behind me," she said to the girl without taking her eyes off them.

"Mommy, those people told me to let them inside!"

"Who are you two?" The woman demanded. Sofia took a small step forward, but the lady shrieked at her. "Stay back!"

After that last scream, Hue placed a hand on Sofia's shoulder. He'd just experienced long sessions of violence. He didn't want to feel another one.

"Take it easy," he muttered. "My name is Hue. I know you want to protect your kid. My mom would've done the same to me." Hue felt a gnawing sensation in his heart. The words he said were a half-hearted lie. His mom would've done the same for him only before she remarried. His words didn't seem to reach her. The woman wouldn't let her guard down.

"What's your name?" Sofia asked, trying to defuse the tension.

"You first." The woman shoved her daughter behind her legs.

"I'm Sofia." She and Hue kept their distance, while Heather's mother eyed them both.

"I'm Lisa." She then kept her mouth shut as if refusing to say more. "There, you know who I am. Now, you can leave." Heather hugged Lisa even tighter.

"I'm sorry, but in case you haven't noticed, there are monsters outside," Sofia said. She did her best to keep a steady voice, but the act seemed nearly impossible. Heather's frazzled blonde hair and teary eyes didn't help to ease her fear either.

"So, you've run into them as well?" she asked. This time, Hue stepped in.

"Yes," he said, nodding.

"Mommy, if they're running from them, does that mean they're the good guys?" Lisa shushed her before commanding her to squeeze herself into the corner of the room. "What are we going to do?" Heather whimpered. Lisa turned to Sofia without answering her daughter's question.

"So, where did you come from?" she asked.

Sofia stuttered before finally letting the words out. "I was driving with my mom before we crashed our car." She made sure not to mention exactly where she was from. If Hue came all the way from Iowa, there's no telling where Heather and Lisa came from. More confusion would only wreak havoc on them. For all she knew, they might've been from the east coast, or even a different country. Lisa moved her long hair out of her eyes. She and Heather bore the same facial features, and they stared at Sofia with a piercing gaze.

"So, since you said you were driving with your mom, I'm assuming you're looking for her?" Sofia nodded. Even Hue took the time to nod in agreement. Lisa eyed him. "Don't you dare go near my daughter!" She changed her tone of voice just as quickly as she changed the subject. Her glare scolded them. Hue didn't argue. Instead, he backed up as though he were scared.

"All we want to do is get to the hotel," Hue said. "Sofia got a voicemail from her mom. She told her to go there. She and the other townspeople were waiting out the blizzard together."

Lisa scoffed at him. "You two have never been here, have you?" She slowly brushed past them. "Everyone knows some cult runs this town, and that hotel is a breeding ground for initiating new members." Sofia and Hue looked at each other. She considered the horrors they had witnessed so far, so the idea of a cult didn't seem too far-fetched for such a strange town. Hue just folded his arms across his chest. Still, he offered no argument.

"Yes, my mom's been looking into that." Heather's frail voice suddenly came to light. She stood steadier in their presence. Her legs no longer shook, and she made eye contact with them.

"How do you know about this?" Sofia asked Lisa.

All of them ignored Heather. Lisa rolled up her right sleeve to reveal a raven tattoo on her wrist.

"When Heather said I was looking into this cult, she meant it. I became an initiate to see if they'd show me their secrets. I knew something was wrong with a good portion of the people in this town. And when one of them had the audacity to ask about Heather, I snapped. But I didn't want to immediately accept the notion a fully-fledged army of fanatics lingered in the town." Sofia took another long look at her tattoo. The raven's feathers came straight out of her skin like it was alive.

"Okay then," Sofia muttered and pulled out the drawing Charlie gave her. "Is this woman and these men part of the cult?" Sofia held it in front of Lisa's face. The woman ran her fingers across the drawing. Her digits flowed down Dabria's entire image, and although it was a simple sketch, Sofia still felt like those red eyes could jump out at Lisa anytime.

"Yes, I know her. Dabria leads the damn group, and those two men are just a couple of boys she plucked from the high school. I swear. . . she has a creepy obsession with indoctrinating broken children." Lisa took a deep breath. The air beneath her lips wavered, and Sofia felt the dread exuding from her mouth.

"I saw her on the road before my mother crashed the car," Sofia said.

Lisa shook her head. "If she's up and about, then we need to get out of this town as soon as possible. This doesn't happen often." Lisa went to the corner and took Heather's hand. Hue felt off about what Lisa said. Why did she talk like Dabria was long forgotten? He saw her actively trying to influence him. "That voicemail you got," Lisa said to Sofia, "It must be a trick. Dabria just wants to catch you off guard." Sofia whipped out her phone while simultaneously shoving the drawing back into her pocket. Lisa pointed to the cell phone with a confused look.

"It's my cellphone," Sofia muttered.

"I've never seen one without any buttons." Sofia scratched her head. She just assumed that it was because Lisa was an older woman, but even Heather looked at it fascinated while Hue tilted his head like he was lost. After all, Heather was young enough to grow up using the technology. "It doesn't matter," Lisa said, interrupting their thoughts. "Just know that whatever message you received, that couldn't have been your mom." Lisa gently took Heather's hand before walking out of the bedroom.

"I guess they've been living without cellphones," Hue muttered sarcastically. Sofia's heart fell. She was hoping they'd have an extra battery pack to charge the device. Now, even her only hope of contacting her mother vanished.

"Well, are you coming?" Lisa asked from the hallway. She peeked her head back into the room. Sofia saw Heather's shadow peering in. Hue sighed. He nodded to Sofia as a silent gesture to just follow Lisa. He strode into the hall.

"No, wait!" Sofia stammered. "We can't just assume the hotel is a trap! We have to find my mom!"

This time, Hue didn't reinforce her comment. Nor did he act in the same heroic way he did earlier. "Sofia, after everything that's happened, do you honestly think that we can even move around this place without being slaughtered? With all those monsters running around, how the hell are we supposed to stay safe?" Hue asked. Sofia pursed her lips. The beating of her heart pumped blood through her body. Just earlier, Hue did everything he could to protect her. She'd clung on to him too quickly. His disagreement put them at odds.

"But why should we trust Lisa?" Sofia didn't hesitate to blurt out her question, hoping it would disarm him.

Hue glared at her. "She seems just about as torn up about this place as we are. Plus, it's obvious we can't fight off these things on our own. I'd say we just leave and come back when we're ready."

He turned on his heels, firmly planting his foot into the wooden floor as he reached the door frame. "No." Sofia snapped. "Obviously, she's been here longer than we have. She'll tell us how to get out of here." This time, her face scrunched up. And as Hue looked at her from his position, she heaved a deep sigh. His adamant nature and the sound of the girls downstairs only forced her to agree.

"Fine," Sofia said with disappointment. She followed him into the hall, and they descended the steps.

"Don't worry. Once we get out of here, we'll figure out how to save your mom." Hue only said the words he knew Sofia wanted to hear, and she sensed his deceit. Just like her mom, he broke her heart.

"Remember, the cult runs deep within the bloodline of most families within this town," Lisa said. The two of them came to an abrupt halt. Her ramblings about the cult started just as soon as they reached the first floor. All three of them stared at each other while Heather gazed into the outside world. "Anyway," Lisa continued. "Even though there's plenty of them out there, I don't think they have a big enough group of extremists to control everything. Once we get out of here, we'll never run into them again." Hue gave off an aura of confidence, unlike Sofia. Lisa spoke as though she never planned on returning to the town, but Sofia wanted to do the opposite.

"And what about those monsters?" Sofia asked.

"What?" A few shots of saliva flew through Lisa's lips as she quickly expressed her confusion.

"The monsters. You're forgetting those monsters. Won't they stand in our way?" Lisa waved her off dismissively. "Hey, you're not listening!"

Sofia marched toward the woman, only to be stopped by Hue. He quickly held onto her forearm.

"Just stop for a moment, both of you." Hue stomped his foot into the floor and used his body to create distance between the two. "Let's just focus on getting out of here first." Hue sounded firm, just as Sofia expected. After all, he didn't hesitate to ditch the plan of finding her mom. "Everyone here should start making up a plan. I'll get that umbrella first. Any weapon would be a good one at this point." Sofia nodded. Even though she felt disappointed in him, his strong will still had a charm to it. As soon as he disappeared up the stairs, Lisa came back with a book presented in front of her.

"Here. I've kept this on the shelf for ages." She handed it over. The large leather-bound cover sunk into Sofia's skin. "This 'book' is what the cult would consider to be their own bible. Since you still need to be convinced of how dreadful this place is, I suggest you read a few pages." Lisa's tone remained sarcastic. It became a part of her personality as much as Sofia's ignorance was to her. Suddenly, Hue reappeared with the umbrella along with a small backpack.

"These should be useful!" When his foot left the last step, Heather made eye contact with him.

"Hey! That's my bag!" She pouted.

Lisa turned to her. "Quiet! We don't know what's still hiding outside. Just let them take what they need and behave!"

Heather's face softened despite her mother's harsh tone. She squinted at Hue. He gave an awkward smile, hoping it would ease the tension.

"That's great," Sofia said. Hue went over to the kitchen to loot more supplies. As he rounded the corner, he bumped into Lisa standing in the pantry.

"Sorry," he muttered.

"You have more sense than that girl," Lisa said. "Just take what you need. We have duct tape and other junk. Just be creative." As she hissed at him, Sofia's ears picked up on their conversation. For the most part, she was left unfazed, but she didn't let that distract her from reading the cult's bible.

For the good of all people, one child shall suffer the burdens of eternal flame. From that flame will rise a new world. A world filled with mortal strife. A world that separates the fools from the profound. The good from the evil.

Sofia's eyes narrowed on the cryptic verse. Each passage had a clearly defined number by it, along with the chapter name at the top. She just read a quote from 'Dabria one, verse eleven.'

"Lisa," she said, clutching the bible. The young mother came back to answer her call. "You said you were initiated into the cult. Do you know what this quote is talking about?" Sofia kept her finger on the passage while Lisa approached. The woman's eyes moved back and forth across the page. She whispered the words to herself, showing a deeper expression of dread with each sentence.

"That's something I've been trying to remember. At some point, I forgot everything. But it's probably better that way."

"What do you mean?" Sofia pressed her face closer to Lisa's.

"Get back!" Lisa nudged her away. "I just forgot about most of this after some big congregation the cult held. I know this quote meant something awful. Maybe that awful thing just made my brain choose to forget." Her voice sounded like she was gasping for air. As if she could inhale bravery to kill her desperation.

Sofia shook her head. Just when she needed more answers, Lisa conveniently mentioned that she had forgotten the important pieces of their puzzle. Perhaps it was the town itself. It seemed so alive like it was trying its best to keep its secrets hidden.

"We need to find out," Sofia said.

"No! We're getting out of this town. I'm not letting anything slow us down!" Lisa talked down to her with the same condescending tone as Sofia's mom. The brutality in her words made her clench the bible tightly to her chest. Out of the corner of her eye, she noticed Hue walking toward them.

"How about you two stop arguing and get ready to leave? If we learn anything on our way out, we'll just make sure to remember it." Sofia wanted to shove him. Even though he tried to please both of them, she knew it was only so they could get out as fast as possible. Eventually, Heather walked up to Hue. She pulled on his sleeve. "Oh, right!" He knelt to her height and unzipped the bag. She poured small snacks, water bottles, and a few rags for them to keep. Afterward, Hue sealed it. The little girl went to the kitchen and returned with a giant knife. "Be careful with that," Hue warned.

They all watched as he used duct tape to attach the knife to the tip of the umbrella.

"Thanks," he said.

Sofia watched him pat Heather's head. The girl gave a smile while Lisa softened her facial expression.

"I have these too!" Heather proclaimed. On the coffee table behind them were broken-down cereal boxes. Hue didn't hesitate to tape the cardboard over various parts of his body. Once he was finished, his shoulders, forearms, and shins were covered by the makeshift armor. Sofia eyed him up and down. She marveled at his resourcefulness.

"You're just like a knight!" Heather gave a short laugh, and despite their horrible predicament, her childish innocence made her giggling infectious.

"Well, it's better than nothing." Hue smiled. He maintained a firm grip on his umbrella.

"Let's get going," Lisa said. "There's a massive sewer system out there. We can use the tunnels to get out of here." They stood in line, facing the door. Hue took the lead. With his spear in hand, he walked just as bravely as a spartan warrior. He cautiously led them down the porch. His legs moved slowly like he was traversing a minefield, and by the time they touched the snow, they collectively sighed.

"All right then." Hue took the map. "I see the tunnels. We just have to figure out where we are. After the roads rearrange themselves, I can find a path to get us there." During his short briefing, he led the way.

Chapter 12

The four of them marched through the snow. At first, they wandered, but as Hue and Sofia began to recognize the roads, their journey started to look brighter. Sofia would turn around to glance at Lisa occasionally. Her attitude never changed—always the brutish mom she was. The houses faded into the background, and eventually, the blizzard started again. Hue raised his hand. At his signal, they stopped.

"Please don't separate us," he whispered silently to himself.

Sofia heard the desperation in his voice but decided not to comment on it. Within only a minute, the world became clear again. Even though she felt betrayed by the fact he wanted to leave her mom, Sofia still appreciated his altruistic actions. They made her feel safe, similar to when her father shielded her from the world.

"Where are we now?" Sofia leaned over Hue's shoulder. He already had the map up to his face. Her eyes watched him drag his index finger around the map.

"Hold on a minute." He remained steady. Ahead of them, the roads returned to their rightful place. They contorted themselves into the same position as shown on the map. Sofia's eyes glistened. To her, looking at the road felt like an entrance into hell. With this new revelation, she knew it would be time to leave her mother behind. But to Hue, the path to heaven was paved right before them. "That's it." He put the map back into his pocket.

"Did the roads go back to normal?" Lisa asked.

"Yes." Without a hint of hesitation, he pressed forth.

"Let's not waste time then," Lisa said.

The uneasiness within Sofia buckled down into the depths of her stomach. She braced herself for the mental turmoil that was to come next. As the rest of the group agreed on getting out, she dragged her feet. The closer they got to the sewers, the harder Heather clutched onto her mom.

"Sofia," Hue said without turning around.

"What is it?" Her voice shook from the cold.

"Back at the house, when we talked about leaving, I meant it when I said we'll come back for your mom." She tried to let his words warm her heart, but the uncertainty of everything put her at a crossroads. Over time, she learned that expecting her wants to be fulfilled only led to disappointment. "I know I wouldn't want to leave Mom in this hell hole. As much as she hurt me, I wouldn't do it." He gave her a side-eye. She believed him.

Those tiny tidbits about his family, is he hiding something? Is he refusing to tell me everything? Sofia let her questions linger inside her.

"You know, after I ran into you, you got upset when I asked about your family," she said.

Hue let out a sigh. "I'm sorry about that. To be honest, I'm just jealous of you."

"What?" Sofia briefly slowed her feet, but when Heather stubbed her toes on Sofia's heels, Lisa shoved her forward.

"Yes," Hue said without noticing. "You were so eager to mention your love for your dad. Not only that, but even your mom held some importance to you." His voice fell as the conversation continued. Sofia took a deep breath. "I wish I could still care about both my parents."

"What exactly happened to you?"

Hue shook his head. "I'm sorry. I shouldn't have brought them up. I guess, sometimes, I just try too hard to relate to someone." He spoke dismissively. Sofia couldn't see his face no matter how much she wanted to, partly because of the snow and partly because he made sure to hide his sadness.

"Right there," Lisa said abruptly. Directly in front of them stood a giant iron gate that smelled of filth. The stench consumed them. Hue took off his pack and handed everyone pieces of cloth. He then tied some cloth over his face. The rest didn't hesitate to follow his example. The makeshift mask put Sofia a little more at ease.

"All right then," Hue said in a muffled voice. He walked forward to the iron door that guarded their exit. He waved his arm, prompting them to all take a step back. He raised his foot to the height of his waist before striking the metal with his heel. In one clean kick, it swung open. Sofia looked at Heather, then to Lisa. Heather held onto Lisa's hand while her mom dragged her along. Even though they clearly discussed their plans, Heather still seemed confused. Hue stepped into the darkness first. Lisa pushed Sofia aside before they all entered.

Sofia thought back to the bible. The town had a lot of history to it. Surely, leaving wouldn't be that easy, right? After being followed relentlessly by monsters and Dabria appearing everywhere, everyone probably wanted them to stay.

"Can you hurry up?" Lisa's strained voice broke through her thoughts.

"Yeah," Sofia mumbled. They walked a straight path through the tunnel. Instinctively, Sofia held her hand out in front of her, but that didn't matter. Their eyes eventually met an orange light.

"Wait." Hue held up a hand. Ahead, the light emanated behind a rock. "All of you, stay here." He ran forward only to realize the light was a torch. Rather than seeing it as a lucky find, he squirmed at the fact that someone had been there. Nevertheless, there was no point in leaving it behind. He picked it up. "Someone, hold this."

Lisa sprinted forward. Heather struggled to keep up, but once the woman took hold of the torch, she smiled.

Sofia dreaded the idea that they'd cross paths with someone else, such as the men from the bible. She still couldn't fathom how the town's cult made such a big impact. Not only that but if they were so infamous, where did they go? She thought back to the quote. *For the good of all people, one child shall suffer the burdens of eternal flame.* Even recalling those words caused her arms to be covered in goosebumps as if that thing came straight out of a horror film. And that new world they mentioned, was it a real place? Sofia shook her head. It was all one big riddle to her. And while everyone became so hell-bent on escaping, she felt like she was the only one trying to solve it.

"Lisa," Sofia asked, trailing behind her. The woman stood side by side with Heather. She slowed her pace enough that she didn't have to drag the girl.

"What is it now?" Her voice was rough.

"This cult. . . what do you remember from when you became an initiate?"

Lisa sighed. "There's not much to tell. They're really just a group of lunatics playing dress up." She raised the torch high over Hue's head. Their shadows danced on the walls. But a glimpse of an apple appeared above Heather. Sofia narrowed her eyes at it. Hue glanced back at her. However, the shadowy image disappeared almost as soon as it entered.

"But there has to be more!" The odd happenings with the shadows. . . It was unnatural.

"No, that's it," Lisa bluntly said.

"But why? With you starting to get involved, shouldn't you have learned more? Didn't they reveal anything to you? Dabria—"

"Enough!" Lisa's voice boomed through the sewers. They bounced off every wall, bringing the entire group to a halt. Hue turned around. Heather kept her eyes on her mother.

"Guys, stop." Hue made a simple command, yet they refused to take it in.

"No! I need to learn more!" Sofia snapped back at Lisa with further questions. "There has to be more about the cult. Surely, it had an effect on your personal life as well! Please, my mom is still out there, and we have a bunch of madmen on the loose!" Lisa grunted. She let go of Heather. The young girl stumbled to the side as Lisa pushed past her.

"Listen, I already told you everything I know!" Every word of hers came out with a shot of spit.

"Well, you told me quite a bit earlier. Don't act so clueless now!" Sofia yelled.

Lisa gripped her collar. Hue immediately stepped in between the two. He stretched both arms to maintain the distance he created.

"Stop!" he yelled. "Let's get out of here first! Then you two can argue as much as you want!" He gritted his teeth.

Lisa turned her head away while Sofia frowned. Through their little scuffle, the flame of the torch almost grazed Sofia's cheek. Hue held his hand. A small burn mark embedded itself into his skin.

"Hue, you're burnt," Sofia said in a soft voice. She tried to examine his injury, but he pulled his arm away.

"Just make sure you two don't fight again. That way, I won't get hurt trying to stop you guys." He marched away, taking his place again as the head of their group.

"I'm sorry," Sofia muttered. Her words didn't reach him. With Lisa giving a look of disapproval, Sofia decided to focus on the tunnels instead. But the deeper they went in, the brighter everything got.

"Something doesn't seem right," Hue said. In front of them glowed an orange light, but the source remained hidden around the corner. Hue kept a close eye on the flickering glow. Suddenly, the shadow of a man was illuminated against the wall. Hue frantically waved his hand up and down. "Put the torch out!" he stuttered. Lisa quickly submerged the flame in the murky water that ran down the center of the tunnel. Just then, other shadows showed.

Sofia squinted to see better. Both she and Hue never broke their gaze. Eventually, the source revealed itself. Around the corner came men in gas masks, followed by Dabria. Before Sofia could even react, Hue shoved everyone into a tiny crevice beside them. They sunk their backs into the stone walls. Lisa put a hand over Heather's mouth. They remained hidden as the cultist passed by. As Dabria grew closer, Sofia closed her eyes for fear of seeing her face. On the other hand, Hue stayed on high alert. He readied himself to see that long hair, red eyes, and emerald broach.

The woman remained enigmatic to them, yet just her mere presence felt like they were being given a presentation of all her horrible deeds. She looked just as she did in their most recent find. The remnants of the little girl she once was still shined, but the raggedness of adulthood was starting to hit her. Hue held his spear close to his chest. The warrior in him was getting ready. He had the same look when the monsters attacked, but getting caught would be a death sentence. When the group finally walked past their crevice, everyone held their breath. Hue peeked his head out first.

Upon looking down the tunnel, he realized they had disappeared. He waved at all of them to come out. Each of the girls let out a sigh of relief.

"We can't let them see us," Lisa said. "The things they do to their prisoners are. . . unpleasant." Sofia locked eyes with her.

"You know what they do with prisoners? So, you do know more about them." She spoke firmly while Heather became sandwiched in between them.

"You two have to stop," Hue lectured. "As far as I see it, Lisa is right. We just have to worry about not getting caught." He stepped toward the path Dabria came from. "They got in here from somewhere. I'll bet there's another entrance close by." Following Hue's lead, they stepped over the rubble. Rats scurried across the ground near the black water. Unlike before, Lisa folded her arms across her chest rather than holding Heather's hand. The girl craned her neck in every direction, taking in the sights.

By now, sweat dripped from Sofia's cloth mask. The prospect of leaving the sewer behind only became more favorable with every step, and she knew the rest of them would agree.

"Mom," Heather said. Lisa looked down at her. "Are there more of them?"

"I don't know." Lisa shook her head.

This time, Heather reached out to hold her. But in her effort to grasp her mother's hand, she tripped. Her tiny body splashed into the water. Hue quickly turned around. He shot his hand deep into the sewage and pulled her out. The little girl coughed loudly, the noise booming through the tunnels. Lisa shushed her while Sofia looked around them, fearing they would be heard.

"Hue!" Sofia whispered. She pointed at an orange light approaching fast. Heather hid behind her mom, Sofia hid behind Hue, and Hue stood in a fighting stance. As soon as the torch holder came close to them, Sofia saw her reflection in the goggles of his mask.

"Hey!" he yelled at them in a muffled voice. Sofia's heart rate rose. His legs moved faster. Hue held his spear, ready to strike a fatal blow, but the man had no fear as he charged forward.

"Hue! Look out!" In a mere second, the man brandished a dagger. He dropped his torch. The light remained in the perfect position for the steel blade to shine. He jumped high in the air, holding the dagger over his head. Before he could land, Hue thrust his weapon up, stabbing him through the torso, just below his chest. For a moment, everything stood still. Hue had fought off the monsters, but this was the first time he killed a man.

All he could think about was his mother's disappointed face and the horrified expression Harry had given him in their last encounter. The cultist stared past Hue right at Sofia. Hue still held the spear tightly. When he pulled his weapon out of the man's body, he shot his leg out. His heel made contact with the stab wound. He fell backward, his robe flowing with the gust of wind.

And as Hue watched the body of his victim flail, he never felt more alive. He felt the same rush of adrenaline when he last saw Harry, and when he fought off the monsters. As bad as their situation was, the strength that flowed through him was something he could look forward to. His mind split in half. One side of him retained the fear he had felt all his life, but the other side felt great to be able to fight back.

Hue screamed and continued his attack. He stomped on the man's chest before plunging his weapon into him.

The robe tore with each successive stab wound, but rather than blood escaping the corpse, air as dark as coal came out and evaporated.

"Hue, Stop!" Sofia pleaded. Ever since they faced the monsters, he'd been pushing himself harder than he needed to. He was trying to bear the weight of the world on his shoulders. "Hue!"

He kept sinking the spear into the man. The coal-colored air continued seeping out, leaving a black mark spread diagonally from the top of Hue's forehead down to his chin. Sofia shook him a few times until he came back to reality.

"What?" he asked, irritated. But regret slowly settled in when he noticed just how much Sofia's fear of him mirrored his mother's. When he looked at Lisa, he saw her holding Heather like a precious piece of treasure. The kid burst into tears while Lisa's stubborn attitude became more solemn. Sofia still held his shoulders. Hue looked down as he dropped his weapon. The spear clashed with the cement. The kitchen knife he taped to the tip resembled a shadow. Hue fell to his knees.

It's just like when we fought. I'm no better than him. Hue covered his mouth with his hand, holding back the urge to vomit. He always swore he'd be the same person he always was. But now, just like Harry, he fell into a deep rage. He had it in him, too. Eventually, he couldn't hold in the little food he had the day he ran away from home. A stream of puke shot out, followed by wails and tears that wouldn't stop.

Sofia knelt to embrace his trembling body. He cried into her shoulder while muttering to himself.

"Not like him. Not like him." Sofia patted his back as he softly spoke. "I'm turning into him." Sofia continued to hold him close to her chest. Through his watery gaze, he saw in her eyes she was tearing apart at the sight of him. However, the sound of multiple footsteps closing in ended their embrace.

"We have to go!" she yelled. Sofia turned to Lisa, who was well on her way to running past them. This time, she carried Heather in her arms. The girl was still crying. "Listen, Hue, we have to go!"

"Sofia, I just. . . I hurt another human being." She grabbed his arm to pull him to his feet.

"Let's talk about that later." She panted rapidly. But despite her rebuttal, Hue remained adamant about being frozen.

"I just killed someone," he muttered.

"You did what you had to do. Come on." She finally garnered the strength to bring him to his feet. "If you didn't stop him, we'd be dead already. I need you to be brave again. Just like you *always* were." They didn't have any more time to waste. From the splashing water to the incessant screaming, they undoubtedly made enough noise for the previous patrol group to hear them.

"Are you two coming?" Lisa asked, turning to them. She made it all the way to where the man came from. She'd crossed that distance as fast as lightning, and Sofia knew she wouldn't hesitate to leave them behind.

"Let's go," Sofia said to Hue. Just as he held her during their first run, she held his hand, bringing him along. But as soon as they reached Lisa, another group of cultists appeared before them. This time, they came in droves. They held no torches. The light from the dead man must've led them there. Lisa hugged Heather to the point she almost suffocated. Hue's pupils grew again. He looked like a drunk man who quickly sobered up.

He suddenly displayed the same hatred as when he killed their previous attacker. They were only worthless insects to him, ready to be crushed. The familiar bloodlust returned to him. A couple of the men charged forward. Sofia ducked out of the way, while Lisa stuck her foot out to trip one of them, clutching onto Heather as she did so. One of the attackers screamed as he fell into the murky water. Meanwhile, Hue dodged blows from everyone who threw a punch at him. And each time they missed, he counterattacked.

He may have looked like a battered dog, but he fought like a lion. However, their numbers overwhelmed him. Once his knuckles were bruised and black from knocking a few of them out, they piled on top of him. Two men held his arms while a third used their foot to hold his face to the ground. Hue grunted and rolled, but no matter what he did, he couldn't escape.

***

When Sofia ran to his aid, they shoved her back. She fell flat on her bottom while another patrol came in from the rear, bringing Dabria along. She stood behind the group of men that passed them previously. As Hue and the girls were apprehended, their wrists were bound behind them by rope. After that, the men parted like the Red Sea. Their actions made way for Dabria to walk forward. The tip of her blue dress was wet with filth. She looked down at Sofia, who had already been brought to her knees.

"Finally," Dabria said.

Sofia looked at her face. "You. You're the reason my mom crashed her car." She tried to wiggle out of her captors, but her resistance was met with a kick to her mouth.

"Relax, you're here to be reformed. If you manage to leave this town, you'll be an even better person than you were before." Sofia narrowed her eyes on her. Dabria spoke like a snake. "You seem confused."

Dabria mused. She knelt and held Sofia's chin between her icy fingers. "Both you and that boy over there are here to be given a second chance. An opportunity for redemption. An opportunity that I have rarely given to others." She side-eyed Hue before returning her attention to Sofia.

Beside them, the men tightened black bags over Lisa and Heather's heads. And while they were separated, Lisa fought back as hard as she could. She tried to shake off the strong arms that restrained her. She even managed to butt her head against a few of them.

"Let me go!" she screamed.

"Mommy!" Heather's voice cracked as she called out. Sofia imagined how much the girl must've been crying under her bag. Certainly, the fear that consumed her was like a parasite eating its way out. Perhaps it would've been similar to the time she spent in the court when her mom took custody of her.

"Tell me, child," Dabria said, placing a hand on top of Sofia's head. "Do you seek forgiveness from the one you've wronged?"

Sofia ground her teeth together. "I don't know what you're talking about." She fantasized about breaking free and strangling Dabria until she let out her last breath. But the woman dug her nails into her skin like vulture talons. After that, she forced Sofia's face down.

"I feel sorry for lost souls like you. There's already so much evil in this world. It's a shame you must be cleansed." She took a deep breath. "The air in this town is so corrupted, my followers must wear gas masks. Otherwise, their lungs will be tainted. Both of you must be used to being so evil." Despite his uncomfortable position, Hue managed to let out a grin.

"If we're evil enough to breathe this air, what about you?" Hue asked with sarcasm. "You're not wearing a mask either. What makes you any different from us?" Sofia saw Dabria's heels make their way toward Hue. The woman raised her right foot and slammed his face into the ground. He let out a grunt. And a cut formed at the top of his scalp. This time, Hue made sure to keep quiet.

"And you should know that I only hurt sinners directly if they're absolutely atrocious." Dabria raised her nose high in the air. She looked down at them like they were dogs. Eventually, she motioned her men to lift Sofia to her feet. They escorted her past Hue in the direction where they took Lisa. Now, Dabria kept her full attention on Hue.

"You're the farthest from innocence out of anyone here. I gave you a chance when we first met, and you threw it away," Dabria whispered in his ear. Again, her words felt like a serpent's tongue touching his skin. Hue tried to break free. He almost managed to throw a punch at her, but his actions were met with a hard kick to the stomach. He grunted and coughed. "Such a violent boy filled with hatred. Tell me, does that hatred stem from the influence of your stepfather, or is it pent-up rage held against your mother?"

"You bastard!" Hue struggled even more. But that just prompted the men to tighten their restraints. Another one joined in by holding his ankles down. Hue took in what she said. Even though the old crone spoke in vague sentences, he couldn't deny that he had a strong sense of bloodlust buried within him. His actions earlier were far more extreme than anything else he had ever done. "Once I'm free, I'll kill you." His voice came out as a low growl.

He and Dabria held eye contact. She ran a finger down his cheek.

"You poor boy. Such a fine young man who's been tainted. Not only that, but you're someone who's tainted himself. But you still have a chance to do right." With a wave of her hand, they forcefully bagged his head and Sofia's. Hue felt himself being lifted off the ground. As they pushed him forward, he brushed against Sofia.

"What do you want?" she asked Dabria. Sofia's lips trembled. Her arms became sore from the upward pull the men did to her.

"I fear that boy may never recover from his sins. But you, on the other hand, think with your mind, rather than your fist. Maybe if you think about your mother, you'll realize she's not the woman you believed her to be." Sofia shook her head under her bag.

"Don't talk about her," she said in a muffled voice. Dabria put her hand under her bag. Her skinny fingers trickled up the side of Sofia's face like a spider. At first, she didn't resist, but as soon as Dabria touched her hair tie, she bit down on her finger. Immediately, the woman retracted her hand.

"Your parents have attributes you failed to see," Dabria spoke calmly as though the bite never happened. "Hopefully, your insightful nature will help you see that."

After that, nothing else was said. Hue trudged forward, occasionally clashing the side of his foot against Sofia, but each time he did so, she didn't say anything.

After a few more minutes of walking blindly, they heard a metal door slowly swing open. Hue couldn't see the area before him, but he could feel the icy winds stinging his hands. Even the snow went above his shins. Hue felt a large foot push him, and he smacked the ground. Before he could register what had happened, hands pulled up his torso, bringing him to his knees. Sofia had a more graceful landing when they simply shoved her. Hue uttered cusses to the men until he felt a metal object strike the back of his head with the same intensity as lightning striking a tree.

***

Sofia heard Hue's body flop. She quickly started wiggling her body. She tried to stand but ended up being knocked onto her side. Her body felt hot in the snow.

Did they kill Hue? Was it just one hit, or were they beating his skull into the ground?

"Soon, you will be cleansed," Dabria said, and while her cryptic message lingered in her head, Sofia felt the hard swing of a metal pipe strike her temple. The pain only lasted for a split second, as it didn't take long for everything to fade away.

Chapter 13

Hue had already been awake for the past hour. The cold cement floor enveloped him for so long that his legs had gone numb. He turned his attention from the bars of their cell and back to Sofia. Her head hung to the side as if she were dead, and if it weren't for her soft breathing, Hue would've assumed she was. Just like him, they restrained her. The only difference was that she sat in a chair.

Sofia woke up, looking very confused. Her eyes still needed to adjust to the barely lit room. It had taken Hue a while to get used to it, so he understood what she was going through. Faint footsteps sounded outside their cell. The coldness of her metal binds hit almost as hard as the snow outside, but the blood dripping off her seat felt warm. Sofia finally spoke when she looked at Hue.

"Hue! Hey!" she said. He quickly locked eyes with her and forced out a smile. Her lips weakly parted ways before her eyes wandered. Hue followed her gaze to the dirty sneakers at the back of the room.

"Sofia, I'm sorry." It pained him to look at her face. If he hadn't lost himself in the sewer, they could've run away after killing their attacker.

He stood but couldn't move more than a couple of feet. The chains weren't long enough.

"When did you wake up?" she asked.

"Probably about an hour ago. I've been losing track of time, though." He looked past the bars again. "I keep hearing muffled voices coming from the halls. I don't even remember getting here. They must've knocked both of us out."

Hue looked around. The dim torch didn't offer much to help, but the room reminded him of a medieval dungeon.

"We need to find Heather and Lisa. Then we can go," Sofia whispered. Her soft voice held an undertone of panic.

Hue sighed. She was right. He barely knew them, but leaving behind a little girl didn't sit well with him.

"I've been trying to figure out how we'll do that," he said, looking at the ceiling. "I think I might be able to slip out of these cuffs. I just need something I can use as lube." Sofia's eyes drifted toward the blood scattered across the floor. At this point, most of it had already dried, but Hue could see a morbid plan forming in her mind. She looked at a broken piece of wood sticking out of her armrest.

"If I bleed, do you think my forearm would be slippery enough to escape?" Hue gave her a long stare. He'd only known her for a day, but she didn't come off as a masochist.

"Please don't do that," he begged. "If anything, I should be the one to do whatever it takes to escape." Sofia's expression softened. In stark contrast to his rage-filled murder, he went back to an altruistic state of mind. He even went as far as to pull against the chains.

"Don't push yourself too hard," Sofia said.

Hue ignored her. "There's no need to be so protective of me. I'll do whatever it takes to get everyone out of here." He kicked the base of the chain to no avail.

"You're quite a handful. By the way, those things Dabria said to you. . . About your stepfather, do you know what she was getting at?" Hue turned his face. He already knew he had hatred because of his home life, but he couldn't answer Dabria's question. Where and who was the source of his anger?

"I honestly don't know."

Sofia pursed her lips. "Okay then." She didn't seem satisfied, but let the conversation go for now.

"Let's just focus on getting out of here first." When Hue looked back at her, their moment of bonding was cut short by the men standing at the front of their cell. One of them pulled out a set of keys that clattered against each other. As soon as they unlocked the gate, they made a beeline toward Hue.

"Get away from me!" He tried to throw a kick, but they shoved him down. And again, he found himself on the receiving end of multiple blows to the face. After the longest twenty seconds of his life, one of his teeth came loose from his gums. A warm metallic taste filled his mouth and he spat out a few drops of blood. Just when he thought they'd stopped, he took one more hit to the head. With his world spinning, they dragged him out of the room. Sofia left the corner of his eye as soon as two more men entered the room.

Hue's wrists were sweaty from their firm grips. They dragged him for an agonizing eternity before they thrust him into another cell. Here, only mirrors surrounded him. Both captors stood guard by the exit. Once he regained his composure, Hue contemplated diving in for an attack, but he stopped when he saw himself in the mirror. His reflection looked back at him. He finally saw how ugly he looked. The bloody mouth, black eye, and cut lip. It looked too much like the year after his mom married Harry. Then, the memories flooded in.

There he was, sulking on his couch, his mom blind to the fact that she allowed the incarnation of Satan to enter their lives. Hue was much smaller. At fourteen years old, he hadn't reached his full height. He stood only at five feet two inches and ninety pounds. Harry towered over him, his voice berating his ears. He spat nothing but obscenities in Hue's face. Apparently, his mom didn't scrub the bathroom floor that morning. Hue knew she was still in the house. She never came downstairs to check on them. He bit down hard on his lip. His crumpled shirt already had a few tears from the scuffle with the boys at school. He fought tooth and nail just to make it home, but his only sanctuary harbored a violent father and an absent mother. Who was worse? Hue didn't know.

"Scrub harder." Harry's deep voice never failed to sound threatening. It didn't matter what the topic of conversation was. No matter what he said, it always sounded like a threat. Hue vigorously moved his arms up and down until his skin felt raw. His forearms ached, but his stepfather breathing down his neck compelled him to work even harder. "Pathetic. Even your mom gave you an ugly name." Hue stopped. "That seems to bother you." Harry laughed. He always made fun of Hue's real name. "What kind of woman names their son 'Hubert' anyway? Sounds like something from an old cartoon." Hue's hands gripped the sponge tighter.

His arms shook as he held back his anger until, eventually, he couldn't anymore. He turned around and chucked the yellow sponge at Harry's face in one swift motion. The soap seeped into his eyes.

"You little—" He couldn't even finish his sentence. The soap stung his eyes. Despite successfully hurting him, Hue didn't see it as a win. Harry would get back at him—make sure he'd feel a pain that would make the soap seem like only a pinch in comparison. Hue got up to run but tripped on the bucket. The entire bathroom floor turned into a flooded landscape. It soaked Hue's shorts. Harry picked up the bucket. The last thing Hue saw was the pail flying at him. Once it slammed into his eyes,

Harry covered Hue's face with his palm. The world went dark for him. But the water flowing against his back, his muffled screams, and hits to his body remained. In the end, he lay there after the beating. Harry stormed out of the bathroom, leaving him behind.

After the events of that memory washed away, Hue returned to reality. He stared at the mirror. His face disgusted him. Just when he was about to retreat, one of the men walked forward with a stick. Hue braced himself for another beating, but instead, he jumped at the sound of glass being smashed. Rather than striking him, the man broke the mirror.

"Remember what Dabria said!" the man yelled. Hue flinched again. That woman kept reminding him of his turbulent home life. He didn't want to delve deeper into it. He'd made the right decision to run away. That dealing with Harry didn't just save him, but his mom as well. The man grabbed Hue by his hair and forced him to look at another mirror. "What do you see?" he yelled. Hue ground his teeth together. He didn't want to go down memory lane again. He clenched his hands into a fist. "Do what's right. Let Dabria's justice fix you. Admit your wrongs," the man hissed.

Every muscle in Hue's body tensed. That word 'justice.' It was an ugly word. To his mom, what Harry did to him was justified. Apparently, he was only turning Hue into a responsible man through harsh discipline. Who was Dabria to tell Hue that his actions against Harry weren't justified?

"Justice?" Hue whispered. "Punishing a boy for fighting against his abusive father isn't justice!"

"You insolent brat!" The man yelled. While he continued to tug at Hue's hair, the other cultist stood idle, and Hue could tell he slightly turned his head away.

Hue bit the hand that pushed him around. "Hey, you!" he yelled to the one standing by. "You don't seem as crazy as your friend here! Why don't you tell me why you're doing this? Why is Dabria so important?"

"I- I. . ." The man pinched the side of his robe as he struggled to speak. Despite failing to form complete sentences, the words he did speak held uncertainty. Hue waited for him to form a response, but when his body shifted, Hue noticed that he wore sneakers rather than boots. Not only that, but a small sticker of a pink starfish lay on top of his right shoe.

"Who are you?" Hue asked, dumbfounded. "Do you actually believe in Dabria, or are you some kid just like me?" Once his questions started to instill fear into the man, his partner began physically abusing Hue again. He looked down at him. The surge of power Hue felt in the sewers returned to him. *No point in asking questions.* He wanted blood. If they were a part of Dabria's strange religion, he wanted them to feel his pain. Hue turned in a circle. He kicked the man in the side of the knee. Hue's shin broke right through the cartilage. He went down screaming. When Hue mounted him, the other cultist was already sprinting forward. "No." Hue knew he couldn't take both of them. That's when he remembered what Dabria said about the air.

Her men couldn't stand it. So, Hue ripped off the man's mask. Black smoke came out of his mouth and evaporated into the air. This time, Hue managed to move his face away just in time to miss it. But before he could get off his lifeless body, the other cultist tackled him to the floor. Hue did everything he could to make sure his back didn't meet the concrete. He punched, kicked, and threw his body all over the place. Much to his relief, he found himself on top. He didn't hesitate to rip the guy's mask off. Again, black smoke escaped his mouth.

Hue stood and shuffled away from them with his chest rising and falling to the deep breaths he was trying to take. He let his fingers touch the shards of glass. He just wanted to feel something. Anything that would help him ground himself. To calm down. But calmness wasn't for him. His eyes darted to the first one he killed. He grabbed the man's stick and swung it at a random mirror. The thing broke in half as the glass hit the ground. He needed something else to take his anger out, but he regretted breaking the only thing he could use as a weapon. In the end, Hue turned to the door to return to Sofia.

Chapter 14

After they dragged Hue out, two more men walked inside. Sofia looked at them. Her mind conjured scenarios of pain. Would they beat her just as they beat Hue? One man held a bowl of incense while the other cradled two lit candles. Even though they wore masks, Sofia swore she caught glimpses of their faces underneath. The skin over their eyes was covered in burn marks. And for a moment, the sound of glass smashing came from a room further away. What was happening to Hue?

Please, fight as hard as you can. Sofia's inner voice spoke as if it could reach out to his ears. He was a fighter. He had spirit in him, but if they destroyed that, would Sofia even have a chance of retaliating?

"What are you doing?" she asked in a wavering voice. One of the men held her shoulders to the back of the chair while the other un-chained her. "Stop!" She kicked and screamed, but her fragile frame was no match against their heavy-set bodies. As they dragged her along the floor, she felt the blood that stained the ground. The red splotches had dried but peeled off the floor. Crimson particles touched her skin.

As they pulled her out of the room, she found herself in a long hallway. It stretched in a straight path that seemed perfect for an escape.

A simple route that was easy to follow, but the hands that crushed her skeletal arms crushed her dreams as well. They took her to a vacant room. Hue's screams sounded closer now. The room they forced her into had similar torches and stone walls as the last, but this time, a dark painting with a black frame of Dabria covered one side of the wall. The men shoved her against it while spreading her limbs until her body resembled a starfish. She was chained again. She couldn't help but think of all the possible ways Hue could have been abused, but instead of revealing a torture device, they lit incense.

They then placed a bowl directly in front of her and a candle on each side. The cultist kneeled beside her. She heard their soft prayers kiss her ears, and as the mumbling continued, the incense came closer. She inhaled the scent. Then, the painting of Dabria turned three-dimensional. She knew it was painting, but she swore, it looked just as real as the men there.

Take a trip down memory lane. She heard Dabria's voice again but couldn't find her.

***

Back when she was only seven years old, her father held a barbecue. Sofia had to stand on her toes to see the meat on the grill. Her dad had laughed at her a few minutes before. According to him, her resentment toward an inanimate object was just too funny not to laugh at. To her, being short felt like the world shattered right in front of her face. So, for now, she crouched in the corner of her backyard. She held a steady grip on her tiny shovel and dug out a hole. She already placed a small box down. As a child, the idea of a time capsule intrigued her. Waiting for even a week tested the limits of her patience at her young age, and she vowed to wait at least a few months, this time.

She did a short fist pump. Her new promise to have more restraint exhilarated her, but in her struggle to dig the hole, her hair tie almost came undone. She maneuvered her fingers around the back of her head. Her father always did it for her despite his struggles. She didn't mind he always made a mess out of her hair. It didn't matter if he left her scalp looking like a forest; as long as he did it for her, she was happy. But despite being coddled by her dad all day, every day, she decided to give him a break. Doing it on her own made it a little neater, although it remained a mess.

She brought her attention back to the time capsule. Sofia shoveled dirt on top of the wooden box. The smell of her dad's cooking pulled her out of her focus, and she turned around to see him conversing with their neighbor. Plates of large patties were being passed around. She dropped the shovel before running at him.

"Daddy!" Her high-pitched voice gave a yelp. Unlike her mom, he found it adorable rather than annoying. Sofia hugged her father's leg. She wanted to stick as closely as possible to him, but when she saw her mother glaring at them, she knew he had to go.

"I'll talk to you later," he said. "Your mom has something to say." He handed his spatula over to their neighbor. They immediately switched positions. While her dad walked away, the man living next door flipped the patties on his behalf. Sofia, however, couldn't stop thinking about her parents. She sprinted toward the screen door leading into their living room.

"Why don't you help me out? We're drowning in bills!" her mother said to her father. She was going about her usual tirade. Sofia peeked into the house, remaining hidden. As always, he didn't argue back. As Sofia's

eyes locked onto her disappointed mom, she flinched when her mother slapped the kitchen counter. "Come on! Help us!" her mom screamed. "You're so passionate about doing things for yourself. Why don't you ever put that energy into us?" She leaned on the counter. "Do something! Coward!"

Sofia stepped inside, but they didn't notice her at all. Her mom lost herself in her usual rage. Verbally, assaulting her dad had become a common occurrence. After a few more incoherent screams, she stomped forward. She towered over her dad, who was now on his knees.

"You're useless, you know that?" her mother told him. "Who do you think you are? Do you think you're Picasso? That you'll break out as some famous artist? Everything you make is utter horseshit!" She glared at him with balled fists. "That sculpture you made. . . absolutely terrible! And let's not forget about those blobs on a canvas you call a painting! Open your eyes! You're not making any money! I can't be the only one supporting this family!" She retreated to the kitchen and picked up a porcelain cup. Her dad shook his head at her, and she put it down. "You need to help us."

Sofia's father got back on his feet. "I'm taking care of our daughter, and you know that. I'm trying my best to put food on this table." He raised his hands to shield himself, but her mother showed no mercy.

"She only likes you because she thinks you're fun to be around. Well, let me tell you, just because you're the 'fun parent' doesn't mean I'm the bad one. You need to make money! Responsibility is just as important as playing with our daughter!" Sofia's mom sighed deeply.

"Hey, let's—"

"No!" She didn't let Sofia's dad speak. "Give up. You're not Picasso! You can't even make a dollar. Get a day job! At least then you can help support our kid." After all the fighting, they noticed Sofia standing by the door. She froze in place until her dad looked at her.

"*Daddy?*" *She ran toward her father, hugging him.*

"*Of course, you always go to him.*" *Her mom spat out her words.* "*You,*" *she said, pointing at her dad.* "*Sofia looks up to you, so be a good example.*" *She poured herself a glass of wine before chugging it down. Afterward, she marched out of the house, all while Sofia hugged her dad.*

"*Are you okay?*" *she asked him. He didn't answer. Instead, he cried. The tears flowed down his cheeks and dripped off his chin.*

"*I love you,*" *he whispered. When he got up, Sofia kept her eyes on him. He stood tall like a superhero but lacked the confidence to be one.*

"*Mom was yelling about 'responsibility'.*" *Sofia looked up at her father with wide eyes.* "*She tried to tell me about that before. But I don't like it. It makes me upset.*" *Her dad sighed. As a child, Sofia did whatever she could to avoid schoolwork and chores. She admired the carefree attitude her father had. Yet, at the time, she never considered why her mom was the way she was. She just knew her mom only upset her.*

"*Her dad took the newspaper from the coffee table.*" *Sofia watched him skim over it.*

"*What are you doing?*" *she asked. Her dad let a small smile creep across his face.*

"*Remember when I told you to follow your dreams? Well, that's what I'm doing right now.*" *Sofia watched him tear out the advertisements for job listings. Instead, he looked at the upcoming events for art galleries.* "*Just do what your heart tells you,*" *he whispered.*

***

After her thoughts faded away, both of the men got to their feet and walked around her in a circle. The chains that shackled her wrist to the floor held her down like an animal. In the back of her mind, she still yearned to see Hue again. She tried to guess how much time passed, but judging by the fact Hue stopped screaming, she guessed it must've been a while. She realized just how wrong her assumption was when she eyed the candles. They still looked brand-new, with only a tiny puddle of molten wax at the base of the wicks. She let out a sigh. Even time didn't exist in this chamber. Her memories were just so damn prevalent. But when she heard Hue's footsteps approaching, another memory came back.

***

As soon as ten A.M. hit, Sofia sprinted outside to see her dad one last time. Here she was at sixteen. Her mom calmed down a bit. Sofia wished she had done that while they were still married.

"Will you be all right?" her mom asked her dad. A few suitcases stood around his legs as he waited in front of his old beat-up car. This time, Sofia didn't bother having another fight with her mother. Over the years, as Sofia became more invested in her dad, her mom became less invested in her. Every once in a while, her mom nagged her about getting a part-time job, but she only saw it as her mom trying to separate her from her father.

"Don't worry, I'll be back for your late birthday celebration," her dad told her. Sofia kept her eyes looking at the stone walkway. Flowers graced the grass. They were the same flowers her dad immortalized in a painting, and for a moment, she felt peaceful thinking about how pretty it looked, but she didn't feel the same warmth she used to.

"Here, let me help." Her mom assisted in packing the suitcases. Only on rare occasions would they help each other. Just seeing them like that could've been its own core memory. Once they were done, Sofia's dad

slammed the trunk of his car shut. Out of the corner of her eye, she noticed her mom with a somber expression. As though, she was more sad than angry. Unlike the times her mother ground her teeth, the woman looked more, harmless than before.

"Please, don't go," Sofia begged her dad. They held each other close. "I'll do anything to help you and mom." When he left her embrace, he stared into her eyes.

"You know this has nothing to do with you. Even though your mom and I don't love each other anymore, we still love you." A single tear escaped Sofia's eye.

"I know, but I don't want you to leave. Why'd you have to be the one to?" she asked. Her dad sighed.

"It's just the way things are. I'll still visit now and then. And once you're eighteen, you'll have so much freedom. You'd be able to see me whenever you'd like." Sofia went from letting out a few tears to profusely crying. She knew that as soon as possible, she'd leave her mom.

"If I ever visit you, will you let me stay for a while?" He smiled at her and gave her a quick hug.

"Of course I will. When you're an adult, you can go wherever you want." After they let go of each other, they had no more words to say.

"How about you stay here a little longer?" Sofia asked. She looked at her mom, hoping to get her approval. "Right?" she asked her. "We can eat lunch together again. Then maybe we can watch a movie and—"

"Sofia, stop." Her mom quickly put an end to her request. "Your father needs to go, and that's it." Sofia grunted. Seeing her dad go was like having a knife forced into her heart.

"No, I mean it!" she yelled. "Let's stay together for another day! We could even go to that frozen yogurt store. Dad always took me to! I'll pay for all your snacks, I promise!" She looked back at her father, who *averted his gaze. "Right, Dad? We can all go there again?" He held her shoulders.*

"Sofia, listen to me. Your mom's right. I have to leave."

"No, you don't!" She stomped her foot on the ground. Her childlike tantrums surfaced. "Just drive Mom and me around town! We don't have to do anything else! We can just sit in the car and talk!"

"Sofia! That's enough!" her mother yelled. She scolded her.

"Why can't you just make things work? Why'd you have to divorce him?" She shoved her mom. The idea of her falling into the bed of roses appealed to her imagination, but just before she could give another push, her dad pulled her away.

"Sofia, stop!" He said. "It's best if we go our separate ways." Sofia faced him.

"No, you're a good person. You kept us together for such a long time! You don't deserve this!" He leaned forward and kissed her forehead.

"You need to understand that not everything is the way you think it is," he told her. "Remember, even I make mistakes, and I'm not your knight in shining armor. I'm just a human being. A person, just like you." He walked to his car and stepped in. Sofia ran to the driver's side window.

"Sofia, get back here!" her mom yelled. But Sofia ignored her.

"That's not true! All those things mom said about you being irresponsible aren't true! You've always stuck by me whenever I called for you. That man she's talking about, that's not you." She tried to yank open the car door, but he already locked it. He rolled down his window just an inch.

"I promise, we'll see each other again. I'm not going to stay out of your life forever."

"But—"

"Please, step away from the car." Her dad waved his hand to signal her to step back. She did so reluctantly. It felt like hours passed when she watched him drive down the road. Once he finally left her eyesight, Sofia's mom came in.

"Sofia," she said, placing a hand on her shoulder. But Sofia brushed her off. She couldn't bear to hear Mom's voice. Sofia went inside. The couch she sat on beside her dad still looked just as it did when they talked for hours during her childhood. She proceeded to the screen door at the back of their home. She sat in the same spot after every fight. Her head leaned against the frame as she cried. She could feel her mom's presence but didn't dare to look at her.

"Why?" Sofia asked through gritted teeth.

"Listen, your dad and I have our differences. We're normal people who just expected different things from each other." She spoke softly, but Sofia viewed her words as the hissing of a snake. Her mom resembled a slithering animal making its way through tall grass, ready to strike with an aura of deception.

"You're nothing to me. I hope you know that." Sofia's voice was held back by her stuffy nose, but she still managed to get her words out. For the first time since the court hearing, her mom looked defeated.

Chapter 15

The sound of chains clacking together, along with frenzied screams, filled the room. Hue stood over the unconscious body of one of the men, hovering his hand toward the man's face. The noise must have woken Sofia up, as she was now slowly coming to her senses. While the other lay knocked out, Hue's fingers twitched. He unstrapped the guard's mask.

"Hue!" Sofia called out to him. He lowered his fist.

"Are you okay?" he asked. Sofia nodded. Hue searched the man's robes. As soon as he pulled out the large set of keys, he immediately ran toward Sofia. He ran his hands across the chains that bound her to the floor. Just like him, her face looked worse than ever. With her bruised mouth and cut scalp, he shook his head. So much violence caused by these fanatics.

Hurting them is the right thing. Hue thought to himself. The world was wrong, not them.

"Hue, what did they do to you?" Sofia asked once he freed her. She reached out to touch his bruises, but he pulled back.

"Now isn't the time to get touchy. We have to leave." He offered his hand, which she took. After bringing her back to her feet, Hue stepped over the bodies of the men he just brutalized. The way they lay on the floor reminded him of Harry after he got done dealing with him. He tried to shake the idea out of his head but couldn't.

"You can tell me," Sofia said. She alluded to the time they spent separated. Sofia had this look on her face, and Hue knew she felt he was keeping something from her. He sensed his chest tightening. It was the same sensation he felt when he left home. The memory was still fresh in his mind. He slumped his shoulders as they weighed him down. "Hue," Sofia whispered. He snapped his head back to glare at her. She kept her mouth shut.

"We'll talk once we get out of here," he said. Sofia sucked in a deep breath.

"All right then," she muttered. Hue got the impression more than one weighty matter burdened her chest.

Hue maintained his motivation to follow the corridor. The more steps they took, the more he grunted. He sensed Sofia staring at him, but as long as she didn't pry into his well-being, he didn't mind. Eventually, the path turned into a pile of rubble. They found themselves in a decrepit environment.

"At least things are starting to look different," he said. He took one more step before stumbling. Instinctively, he held his hand to his side. His knees scraped the floor as he made a rough landing.

"Hue!" Sofia knelt and raised his shirt. She pulled it up, exposing the giant slash across his ribcage. Hue ground his teeth. "When did this happen?" Sofia asked. She lay him against the wall.

He breathed heavily as she examined his wound. "When I went to get you, those guys put up a pretty good fight. Seeing that blank stare of yours told me you were really in trouble. I acted recklessly." He exhaled.

When Sofia pulled her hand away, Hue's blood stained her skin. She looked around her.

"What are you doing?" Hue watched with confusion as Sofia picked up a small piece of debris. She ground it against the floor until it formed a sharp tip.

"We can't leave it like that." Without saying anything, Sofia cut off her sleeve and a large portion of the bottom of her shirt.

"You don't have to—" Sofia shoved it hard against Hue's torso. He didn't know if she did that purposely to get him to shut up. Nevertheless, the sudden pressure kept him quiet. As the cloth soaked with his blood, Sofia proceeded to tie her sleeve around him to hold it in place. Upon eyeing her work, she realized it was just about as sloppy as her hair whenever her dad did it.

"There," Sofia said. "Just promise me you'll let me help you as much as you help me." She stared right through him.

"Fine." He made sure not to say anything else. And just like him, she offered her hand. After that, he stood, and they walked side by side. "Let's just try not to waste any more time. Heather and Lisa are out there." He looked forward. Not too far from him awaited a metal door. Then, as he ignored the pain, he trudged onward. He placed his hand on the door. Sofia held him up. "Don't worry about me just—"

"Didn't I tell you to let me help you?" Sofia snapped back at him at the speed of light.

He sighed. "Fine." He didn't like being at the center of attention. Whether that was good attention or bad, to him, any attention was unwanted.

Sofia felt the urge to slap sense into him when he went out of his way to push the door open. His arm shook, and he gasped. With her help, they escaped the hall.

"I knew there's something off about you. Ever since the sewers, you've been acting different," Sofia said, as they entered the next room. Hue couldn't bring his eyes to meet her. "After we get everyone else, let's just tell each other everything." Hue couldn't believe how assertive she was, like a lioness protecting her cubs.

"That woman, Dabria, she was right about me being violent," Hue admitted. With the amount of persistence she showed, he just needed to let a few confessions off his chest. "She even called me a murderer." Sofia trailed behind him as they walked across a catwalk.

"But that can't really be true, right?"

"I hurt my stepdad. I don't know if it was enough to kill him, I just know at the very least, he won't be moving his legs that much for the rest of his life." He clenched his fist tighter, not as a reaction to his gnarly wound but to the words that came out of his mouth.

"And what happened to you?" he asked.

Sofia froze in place. "If I open up to you, you're going to have to open up to me."

"I already did. Do you really want to know more? Maybe I'll even give you my school schedule." This time, he took a firm stance to pressure her into revealing her life.

"I saw my parents." Sofia sighed and started picking at her nails.

"And did you see yourself do anything bad?" Hue brought himself to make eye contact with her. She averted her eyes, and her posture became more closed off.

Sofia's eyes frantically moved left and right, as if she were searching for word or trying to escape his confrontation. Or both. "No. Not at all. The worst I saw was me arguing with my mom." Sofia bowed her head. She added in almost a whisper, "But she also wasn't as bad as I remember."

Hue caught wind of her hesitance. "In that case, are you saying Dabria was wrong about you? Are you really not guilty of anything?" Sofia folded her arms across her chest. Hue eyed her. Figuring that she truly was clueless, he decided not to waste any more time questioning her.

***

Sofia was relieved Hue stopped pressing the issue. Her head was already buzzed with all the things she needed to process. They continued their trek across the catwalk. It overlooked the bottom of a church. However, it didn't hold any similarity to any religion other than Catholicism. An altar, along with a row of benches, was located in the middle of the room. Everything seemed typical of a church, except the place lacked symbols for any deity Sofia recognized. Only a massive golden structure in the shape of Dabria's face was displayed on the wall. And when Sofia narrowed her eyes on the podium, the familiar bible of the cult rested upon the clean fabric covering the wood. Dabria's roots ran everywhere.

"Look," Hue whispered. He pointed at a pile of hay hidden behind the podium. On it, Heather slept soundly while a couple of men sat close to her. They both bowed their heads in prayer. The soft mumbling of their voices gently caressed Sofia's ears.

"We have to find a way to get to her," she said. Hue nodded. Since the numbness had fully set in, she had no problem crouching along the catwalk with Hue. They crouched forward until stopping at a spiral staircase. With the men deep in their prayers, Sofia figured they wouldn't notice anyone sneaking up on them. Hue moved faster than she expected. The focused face he had returned. She just hoped that the bloodlust wouldn't consume him again, but she doubted that.

"I'll get the one to her right. You take the one on the left," Hue whispered. He pointed at the two men before slowly making his way toward his target. Hue's legs gave long, silent strides across the room. Meanwhile, Sofia's heart raced at the thought of getting close to them. But with Heather's safety at risk, she knew she had to find the courage to fend them off. While Hue patiently waited behind his intended target, Sofia gave a short nod. After that, Hue wrapped his arm around the man's neck. He tried to struggle, but that only seemed to make Hue more determined to strangle him.

When the other one opened his eyes, Sofia whacked him on the head with the bible from the podium. He toppled over at the force of her swing. Even Sofia became scared at her capabilities. She never thought she could strike someone hard enough to knock them out. Once he hit the floor, it took a moment for Sofia to stop watching him. Hue was on the verge of killing his victim. Sofia couldn't fathom why he deemed it necessary to beat the guy, too.

"Stop!" she said. Her pleas came out like the sound of a crying toddler. But Hue lost himself. "Hue! He's gone! He's unconscious!"

When her words registered in his brain, he looked up at her. The power he felt within those couple of minutes felt like nothing he had ever experienced before. His heart rate skyrocketed just as much when he fought Harry.

"Remember, we're trying to get out of here," Sofia said. She changed the topic, hoping it would keep Hue's attention. After that, he turned around to examine the room for an exit. Sofia shook Heather awake. It took a few tries, but when she opened her eyes, Sofia found solace in her childlike innocence. The sight of her round face became a welcome contrast to Hue's dark actions.

"Where's my mom?" Heather asked, rubbing her eyes.

"We're about to get her." Sofia kept a hushed tone, but when Heather tried to stand, she gripped Sofia's shoulders.

"I feel dizzy," she said.

"Do you remember what they did to you?" Sofia looked up and down her body to check for any physical injuries. Heather's eyes rolled a little. "Do you remember how they knocked you out?"

"The last thing I remember was tasting something bad."

Sofia pursed her lips. Whatever drug they gave her, she hoped it wouldn't kill the girl. Heather coughed before spitting on the ground. Sofia frowned.

"There's a door around the corner," Hue said as he returned. "It's our only way out." He looked at Sofia and then down to Heather. "What's wrong?"

"She's dizzy. She can barely stand." Heather dropped her head when Hue looked at her.

"All right then. Do you want to carry her, or should I do it?" Before he even asked, Sofia made up her mind. He was definitely more capable of carrying her around, but she needed him to defend them whenever possible. Fighting wasn't her expertise. Sofia took a deep breath. Her skinny arms would finally start bulking. She just hoped they wouldn't struggle as badly as they did when she escaped the preschool. She quickly scooped up Heather. Sofia's legs wiggled like freshly cooked noodles, but Hue helped her stand straight. "Are you ready to leave?" he asked.

"Yes," Sofia spoke in between exasperated breaths, but Heather's soft hands gripped onto her. Hue didn't waste any time getting through the door. Sofia eased her circumstances by allowing Heather to ride on her back. The new room that greeted them depicted the same type of dungeon they woke up in. Cells lined the wall, and a faint breeze flowed throughout the room. Sofia closed her eyes.

Lisa, where are you? Sofia asked herself.

The cold stabbed through her skin. But that discomfort was nothing compared to the horrid stench. Rotting food, feces, and dried blood moved around just like rats scurrying across the floor. Hue bravely walked forward, unfazed by everything. In between each cell was a room being held back only by a metal door. It looked as if the place was a mixture of a medieval dungeon and a high-tech security prison. If it weren't for the tiny glass windows, Sofia wouldn't know what each interior looked like.

Most of the time, they harbored absolutely nothing save for the wooden chairs in the middle and a few torn articles of clothing. They were obviously meant to hold captives, as indicated by the shackles littering the floor. As Sofia gave a glance into each room they passed, Hue walked toward the door at the end of the hallway.

Sofia felt Heather moving her neck around. At least the girl was starting to regain more movement. Her legs even rubbed against Sofia's shoulders.

"Just close your eyes," Sofia said, but Heather didn't listen. The thought of the girl being exposed to even more horrors made Sofia want to gag. Still, she hadn't seen Lisa yet, and judging by Hue's somber face, either he found something terrible, or he was making a hard decision.

"I found her," Hue said, wide-eyed. He did his best to keep his voice down. With a wave of his hand, Sofia came to him as fast as possible. The prospect of making more progress toward their escape eliminated her exhaustion. Sofia's adrenaline boost made it much easier to carry Heather. She understood why Hue almost walked past Lisa. Her unconscious body sat very still in a chair in one of the rooms. This time, Heather regained enough strength to look inside the room. Her head made a quick turn. Some of the grogginess wore off. She threw herself back and forth to get off Sofia's shoulders.

"Mommy!" she squealed. Sofia set Heather down before she could throw herself at the door. She also made sure to cover the girl's mouth. Her palms became coated in her moist breath.

"I know you're excited to see her, and we are too, but you need to stay quiet."

They looked into each other's eyes as a non-verbal agreement. Hue gave them a downward nod.

"Now what?" Hue asked. Sofia felt a good amount of movement in Heather's legs. Whatever they gave to her was wearing off.

"Our only option might be to force that door open." Sofia looked down at the lock, but Hue shook his head.

"We have nothing to break through, and even if we did, we'd make enough noise to rattle the place." Hue folded his arms across his chest. "I'll look around the hall. Hopefully, there's another way in." But as soon as he took another step, he tripped over a wooden plank. As he fell to the ground, his shoe hit the bottom of the wall. The wet stone that once barred entry gave way to form a small hole.

"Move," Heather said. While Hue lay on the ground, she crawled over him. Sofia tried to snatch her, but her small frame had already slipped in. Everything happened so fast. Neither one of them anticipated Heather to recover so quickly, let alone crawl at the sprinting speed of a rabbit. Heather unlocked the door from inside, allowing them to flood in. Hue burst in with the quick tempo and silence of a cat. Sofia came in soon after.

Lisa's hands and feet were bound to the chair with rope rather than shackles. A bad image, but not as bad as they thought. Hue examined the knots while Heather held her mom's hand.

"Do you think you can get her out?" he asked, looking at Sofia. Without anything to cut the rope, he figured slim, yet strong fingers could maneuver around the knots quickly.

"Mommy?" Heather said with a trembling voice. The sight of her battered and bruised mother made her cry. Lisa stirred awake at her daughter's whimper. "Will you be okay?" Heather asked.

After the little girl started spewing out questions, Hue showed more humanity again. He rubbed her shoulders. "She'll be fine. We'll be fine," he whispered.

Sofia saw him hug her tightly while rubbing the top of her head. She didn't expect such a thing from him, but then again, she didn't know how much he related to children who lost their mothers.

"Please, be quiet," Sofia whispered. "We still need to remain hidden so we can all get out of here." After stretching her fingers in all sorts of weird positions, the ropes around Lisa's upper body came undone.

"Nothing matters," Lisa muttered. They all flinched when she suddenly spoke. Hue placed a hand over Heather's mouth before she could cry for her mom. Sofia glared at the woman. They didn't get along, but at the very least, she wanted them to work together. "I know what I did wrong. They showed me. Just like they'll show you. I'm not the only one who's still walking around. I'm not the only ghost in this town." Sofia purposely stabbed Lisa's ankle with her fingernail to shut her up.

"Just stop talking until we get out of here." But the woman didn't acknowledge her. Instead, she turned to her daughter.

"What are you talking about?" Hue asked.

"All of us. Me, Dabria, this entire cult, and even Heather, we're all just dead souls wandering the town. I'm just like them."

Hue clenched his teeth. "Just stop talking," he said, but she didn't listen. Lisa slowly cried. Hue relaxed his hand, allowing Heather to get out of his grip. She ran forward to hug her mom's arm. "Heather isn't meant to be here. She doesn't deserve to be here. She's not like us. It's all my fault."

Sofia found it hard to untie the last threads of rope. "Listen!" Sofia snapped at Lisa. "All of us are already confused. There's no need to ramble nonsense!" she muttered. But Heather became agitated, turning into another distraction.

"Listen to me; I saw the past. I saw what I did, and I played a role in creating this hell. Everything in that bible is true. That quote about the sacrifice of a child, it's all true." Her eyes looked down at Heather as she said, 'Sacrifice.' "Their influence spread toward everyone, and they did all they could to achieve their goal. They desired nothing more than to follow Dabria's wish to create hell." Lisa's breath shook heavily. By the time Sofia released her, Lisa's face turned stone cold. Tears still poured out of her eyes, but her face was drained of emotion. "I have to. . . I have to tell you. . ." but before Lisa could finish her sentence, she fell forward on her knees. Sofia rubbed her back, thinking she could provide enough comfort to stop her ramblings.

"Take it easy. They tried to show me my past, too." Sofia spoke softly, but Lisa stayed in her downward spiral. A stream of puke shot out her mouth without warning. At first, it held a brown tone, but the stream soon turned red. And once it ended, she threw up a pile of blood on the floor. Hue lifted her chin to examine her face.

"We need to get her out of here now!" Sofia kept her teeth shut tight in an effort to control her volume. Neither of them could figure out what was happening with Lisa. Both her mind and now her body were in shambles. Sofia separated her from Heather. The girl didn't hesitate to protest, and this time, they couldn't keep her silent. She kicked and screamed, but for now, Sofia didn't hear any footsteps. Hue lifted Lisa to her feet. But upon holding her in front of him, blood poured from her forehead down to her chin.

She shoved Hue away, and he fell on his back. His head ached when it came crashing like a plane into the cobble.

"Mommy!" Heather screamed. She tried to break free of Sofia's grasp, but once she realized she couldn't, she screamed even louder.

"Heather, stop!" Sofia screeched. "We can't waste our time in here!" Lisa's pupils dilated as she broke into a gigantic smile. Her mouth widened, emitting a deep groan as her teeth lengthened and sharpened. Lisa's once pearly whites now resembled those of a shark. Her eyes transformed to a golden hue, and her pupils shifted into vertical slits. Blood covered her face.

"Sofia!" Hue yelled. He jumped on his feet. "We have to run from her!" Lisa was about to turn into some sort of monster. Lisa threw her head back and gave a loud scream. Heather stretched her arm out, but Hue grabbed everyone and threw them out of the room. Heather elbowed Sofia in the stomach, but Sofia only hugged her even tighter to her chest. Hue stepped out to help Sofia restrain her. In the meantime, Lisa kept screaming. The sound of heavy boots grew closer and closer.

A stampede of men came running through the church. Sofia instinctively covered Heather's mouth, but the little girl sunk her teeth deep enough into Sofia's fingers to draw blood. Sofia grimaced as she put in all her strength to hold the girl. Hue quickly shut Lisa's door, leaving her inside as she turned into an abomination. She threw her body against the door with each consecutive slam, spraying blood on the window.

"Stop!" One of the cultists stood in front of them.

"Go!" Hue stood in front of everyone. "I felt a breeze through the door at our end of the hall! Get it open!" Sofia grabbed Heather's arm. She dragged her to the wooden door at the end of the prison. The sound of Sofia kicking down the door and Heather crying on the ground filled the room. Sofia kept striking her heel against the crumbling wood. The creaking of the barricade breaking apart only prompted her to keep trying. Once she finally smashed it open, the cold air struck her face. The familiar snowfall raged outside.

She picked Heather up and threw her onto the snow. She still needed to be shoved, but Sofia didn't have to struggle. The girl's confidence was already wavering.

"Hue!" Sofia yelled, turning around. She saw a man swinging his club at Hue's head.

He ducked. The weapon blew a breeze over the top of his hair. Seeing as how he couldn't win the fight head-on. He kicked the man back before sprinting toward the door of Lisa's room. Instead of throwing herself against the exit, she screamed and slammed her fist on it. Hue took a gamble and quickly let her out. And much to his relief, she got on all fours and pounced on his attacker rather than him. She sunk her nails into the man's shoulders. Hue ran toward the exit, only looking back to see Lisa bite off a piece of the man's neck. Heather stopped crying as soon as she saw what her mother had become. Sofia could tell the girl was stuck in her fight-or-flight response.

Once Hue got outside, he used what remained of the door to block their exit. Heather mumbled nothing comprehensible.

"Come on, let's go," Hue said, almost out of breath. Heather stumbled alongside them through the snow. This time, Hue let Sofia take the lead. He protected the rear in case Lisa jumped out.

"I'm sorry," Sofia whispered to Heather. However, the girl only held a blank stare. They both took her as far away from the church as possible. Hue and Sofia steadied their breathing. Eventually, as they continued their long hike back to town, everyone lost track of time. But once the church was out of eyesight, the town reappeared in the distance.

"Let's stop for a moment." Sofia didn't hesitate to sit on the snow. Hue watched Heather's small hands turn into tight fists.

"My mom," she muttered. Hue knelt to her height, but instead of throwing a tantrum like he expected, she just cried into his chest. Sofia looked at the two of them, not knowing what to do. Once Heather calmed down, she rested her head against Hue. Her shoulders rose and fell along with her chest. The crying ceased, but her hyperventilating didn't. Hue held her until she expended all her strength, and Sofia proceeded to wait.

"Heather," Sofia said, once the girl became exhausted. "I'm sorry."

"No, you're not," she whimpered. "You took me away from her!"

"Heather, did I ever tell you about my mom?" Hue asked. He wasn't exactly skilled at finding soothing words, but Sofia had to admit he tried.

"I don't care about your mom," Heather muttered. But Hue knew that wasn't true. The little girl was just too hurt to be herself, and after realizing that she wouldn't be the same caring and innocent child she was, Hue let out a single teardrop.

"That's okay." Hue swallowed the lump in his throat. "But at least take in some of what I tell you. We can talk while we walk." Hue grabbed hold of her hand. He nodded at Sofia, who took it as a signal to continue their journey.

Chapter 16

At first, only the sound of the wind and pelting snow rang in their ears. Hue did his best not to crush Heather's hand, but with all the commotion, that proved impossible. While Sofia led the way, Hue opened his mouth multiple times, but words wouldn't come out.

Just jump right into it. Don't be a coward.

"I lost my mom too," Hue said bluntly after a fleeting burst of courage. Heather eyed him. Sofia did her best to leave the two alone. Hue looked at Heather for a reaction, but she didn't say anything. Their eyes met for only a moment. "My mom always loved going to the café near our house. Did your mom ever go somewhere she liked?" Hue kept a casual tone, hoping that mentioning things unrelated to their predicament would relieve some tension.

Slowly, Heather's shoulders slumped. Her small body walked at the same pace as him. "My mom always liked going to the hotel. She was friends with the owner there. She even ordered food when she wasn't staying there, just so she could see him," Heather said. Sofia stutter-stepped when Heather mentioned her mother's ties to the place.

"We have to go there," Sofia interjected. "After everything that's happened, we obviously can't just leave."

Hue sighed. He didn't want to accept that she was right, but the idea of what could be in that place chilled him more than the snow. He gave a silent nod, which Sofia returned. After that, he brought his attention back to Heather.

"Sounds like your mom really liked that place." He hummed, showing his acknowledgment through the vibration of his throat. The blizzard clouded their vision. Hue readied himself. He reached out to Sofia and held her hand along with Heather's. He knew the town was changing again. He closed his eyes and took a deep breath.

"Look," Sofia yelped. Her voice broke Hue's concentration. She pointed at the town. They stood atop a hill overlooking the entire commercial area. Cars dotted the sides of the road. The buildings slowly became more abundant, and the streetlights flickered as if they were still remnants of a normal society.

"Heather," Hue began.

"What?" She responded with a voice gentle enough to make Hue think she hadn't lost her innocence.

"Is everyone in this town really, a ghost?" He receded his hand into his sleeve so that Heather wouldn't feel the sweat dripping from his palms.

"No." Heather spoke quickly, but Hue didn't feel any better. After all, according to Lisa, everyone else, including Heather, was a ghost. Perhaps the kid didn't even know she was dead, and if they left the world of the living, were he and Sofia ghosts as well? Hue swallowed the lump that formed in his throat. *No,* he told himself. *I didn't die in a blizzard, and Sofia didn't die in a car crash. We're alive. We're alive, and we're trapped.*

Sofia squinted her eyes. A dog walked across the street. "Charlie," she muttered. A smile slowly crept across her face. Hue stared at her, wondering who she was referring to.

"Let's go," Heather said. Hue looked down to see her tugging on his sleeve. While Sofia was mesmerized by the town's sudden appearance, the little girl kept her attention on the hotel. Her small finger was pointed at their spiraling towers. "Everyone calls them 'Twin Peaks' cause they go higher than the mountains. Everyone knows it."

She obviously knew just about as much of the town as her mom did, but lacked the vocabulary to describe it. Hue wondered if she unknowingly withheld information.

"Let's not waste time then," Hue said. After Heather lowered her hand, he let go of her. She jogged to Sofia and tugged her arm. "Let me go first." Hue's heartbeat at the thought of what may be lurking through the streets waiting for them. He led the way down the hill and managed to keep himself steady.

Once Sofia's foot touched the pavement, she and Heather took a moment to breathe. Hue, however, didn't allow himself any breaks. "Are you okay?" Sofia asked Heather. She nodded. "Don't worry. Once we get to the hotel, we should be fine."

Hue knew what she said was a lie. But then again, they had nothing else going for them. Sofia looked around, searching for something or someone, but eventually bowed her head in disappointment.

"With the size of those towers, we don't need to look for a map." Hue looked back at the girls. "We're going to walk in a straight line until we get to those things." Before anyone could stop him, he marched forth. The sentry in him returned. They kept walking for the next fifteen minutes, rarely exchanging words, and the silence between them became uncomfortable. The church had left them with so many questions. If everyone was a ghost, how'd they all die, and what had Lisa done that was so terrible? Why did she claim to be just as bad as everyone else? Sofia looked over to Hue, but he was lost in the silence. She seemed annoyed with something, but Hue was grateful for the moment of peace. He didn't yet want to break that.

But it did break. Heather halted in her tracks, and Sofia almost tripped.

"Wait," Heather said. Hue turned around. The girl looked past Sofia and straight at him. His lip quivered. Hue was still in a hyper-alert state.

"What is it?" he asked. Heather made mumbling noises. "It's about your mom, isn't it?" Heather nodded. "And I suppose you miss her, right?" Again, Heather nodded. Hue bowed his head. He wished Heather opened up earlier. He gritted his teeth. Avoiding the hotel didn't feel right, but neither did letting Heather wallow in pity. He walked forward and wrapped his arms around her tiny body.

Sofia smiled at his display of affection. "We'll get to the hotel, and we'll be okay," Sofia said to both of them.

"I still wish my mom was here." Hue patted her back. He ran his hand around her back in circles.

"I know. I know you do. I wish I could see my mom, too." When he pulled back from his hug, he still held her shoulders. She looked up at him.

"What happened to your mommy?" Heather asked. Hue sucked in a deep breath. He looked back at the tall towers before bringing his attention back to her.

"I suppose our walk could wait," he said under his breath. "I had to leave her."

Heather's eyes grew wide. "But why? I wouldn't want to leave my mommy."

Hue sighed. "That's great. And I'm sure your mom wouldn't want you to leave her either. But, over time, I didn't know who my mom loved. Her priority became my stepdad, but sometimes, I'd still see her looking at me. She even cried after my last fight with my stepfather. Until then, she felt like a ghost. We lived together, and we spoke to each other, but once I struck down my stepdad, she felt like a real person. It was like. . . she finally acknowledged my existence." His voice trailed off. It wavered under the weight of his words.

"What's wrong with your dad?" Heather asked.

"He's not my dad. He's just my stepfather." Hue gave a faint smile. He didn't know what other expression to show. Sofia walked to Hue's side. She placed a comforting hand on his shoulder.

"He just wasn't a great fit for me," Hue said. "He got along with my mom—at least he did when they first met. But after a while, he resented me, or maybe he always did." Hue rubbed his chin briefly. "My mom left me for him. Probably because she felt lonely. I don't know what angered me more. The fact that he hated me or the fact that my mom chose him over me." Hue let go of Heather's shoulders. He knew his hand would turn into a tight fist, and he didn't want to crush her shoulder blades. "And... on the day I came here, he and I had a fight. I took out the anger I had for my mother out on him. I destroyed everything my mom had."

Heather's attention was on him, and while she listened to Hue's shaking voice, Sofia's eyes darted to his trembling hands.

"What happened when you fought?" Heather asked. When Hue stood, Heather grabbed his sleeve. Sofia's knees cracked when she got back on her feet.

"He acted the same way as I act now," he said, his voice nearly breaking. He wanted to speak about his past, but it was as if his lungs were clogged by water.

"What does that mean?" Heather asked. She pleaded with him to speak. Hue feared he would snap, but he just took in a deep breath to calm himself.

"Parents with bad habits tend to pass it down to their children. I like to think I'm different, but I'm not," he said. After that, he held her hand. He walked forward with Heather by his side. This time, he sandwiched himself in between her and Sofia. For the first time since they arrived in town, he felt warm. Sofia tried to reach for his arm, but as soon as the dog scampered around a stop sign, Hue jumped in front of them. Despite being bare-handed, he got ready for a fight.

The dog Sofia called Charlie slowly walked forward.

"Hue, wait!" Sofia yelled, but he didn't listen. Instead, his eyes narrowed on the dog. Unlike Sofia, Charlie didn't show Hue any compassion. He got low, seemingly ready to spring into the air. He gave a deep growl as he stalked Hue.

"Stay back," Hue whispered to Heather. He stretched his arm out in front of her.

"I said 'stop'!" Sofia broke through his ranks, and just as Charlie was about to jump at him, she stepped in between them. "Stop trying to kill each other!"

Charlie halted at her command. First, Sofia looked at Charlie. "Stop growling and sit down!" Just like a loyal pet, he shut his mouth and stayed still. However, when she looked at Hue, he still had his fist raised. "Hue, please. Just relax. Not every living thing is trying to kill us."

But he kept hyperventilating. Sofia lowered his fist by slowly pushing them down. Luckily for her, the task came easily. Hue gently lowered his guard as she touched him.

"I don't see why I should trust that thing." He pointed at Charlie. His fur ruffled in the wind.

"Because I met him when I came here. Remember when I told you I met a dog at the library? Well, he's that dog." Sofia pointed at Charlie, who was finally acting like a domesticated pet rather than a feral beast. "Listen, he helped me when I got here. He probably wants to help us again." She tried to hold on to Hue's shoulder, but he shrugged her off.

"He's not just some dog. He went out of his way to find you. That's some supernatural stuff going on! He's making moves of his own." Hue glared at Charlie.

"Please," Sofia pleaded with him, but he still stepped in front of her. This time, he made sure to have Sofia at his back. Instead of retaliating, Charlie remained calm, just as Sofia commanded him to. He turned around, walking down the street that led to the left. He didn't seem at all concerned with taking them down a different route. With one glance at his golden eyes, Sofia seemed inclined to follow him. "Hue, let's go." She pointed her head at Charlie.

"What? Why?" They watched his paws leave prints in the snow. Sofia quickly rushed forward, leaving Hue and Heather behind.

"He led me to Twin Peaks after I crashed. He's a good guide!" She could barely speak as she broke into a sprint. Hue uttered a cuss before looking down at Heather.

"Let's go," he said to her. He didn't want to waste any time waiting for the girl to catch up, so he opted to just pick her up in his arms. When they rounded a corner, Hue locked his eyes onto the back of Sofia's head.

"Hey! Do you even know where he's leading you?" Hue called out.

"No!" Sofia yelled back. "But in the time I've spent with him, he kept me alive!" Hue grunted. Following a dog around in a dangerous town with a bunch of people willing to kill them seemed like a horrible joke. But, at the same time, splitting up would be even worse.

"It's okay," Heather said. Hue looked down at her. She wrapped her arms around his neck. "He looked friendly." Hue gritted his teeth. Of course, she thought he was friendly. Children never fail to ogle cute animals.

"You can't trust every dog you see," Hue muttered. As Charlie picked up the pace, both he and Sofia ran faster. Eventually, the strain of Heather's weight became too much for Hue. He only opened his mouth to breathe rather than speak.

"That dog just looks friendlier than other animals I've met. It's like he's a person." Her words didn't register as something he whole-heartedly believed in. He adored her childlike innocence, but risking everything by putting all their faith in an animal crossed the line into stupidity. For a few seconds, he slowed his run into a light jog.

"Sofia, stop!" he yelled. He needed a moment to rest, but Charlie didn't give them a chance.

"We can't!" she shouted back. "Look, he's slowing down!"

Charlie ran through the open door of a bar. Sofia peeked her head in as he sniffed around. Before walking through the door, she beckoned Hue and Heather to enter. Hue came to a halt. He knelt to give Heather an easier chance to touch the ground. As soon as her weight left his arms, he took a deep breath.

"Are you okay?" Heather asked him.

"Yeah, I'm just a little winded. Go in, I'll follow you." As he regained his strength, he noticed a poster just barely sticking to the brick exterior of the bar. The design of a raven with its wings stretched out made a home at the center of the page. The words were torn off, but Hue still recognized the sinister design of the cult. Meanwhile, Sofia paced the wooden floor. The lights hanging above them flickered occasionally. Heather went over to the jukebox under one of the windows.

"What is this thing?" she asked.

Sofia darted her head in her direction. "It's a jukebox. My dad told me how often he and his friends saw it in every bar and diner. He always said it played some of the best songs." The strength in Sofia's voice slowly diminished. A pool table waited in the middle of the room. All the balls and cue sticks were laid by the side as though someone took the time to care for them. It was not hard to imagine patrons sitting around, drinking alcohol from the shelves, by looking at the numerous stools placed in front of the bar. A time before Dabria rose to power. Sofia walked behind the bar as her curiosity got the better of her.

"There's nothing here!" Hue said, stepping in. "I came to this place when I arrived. What does that dog expect to find here?" He watched Sofia explore the tight space behind the bar. Her hands shuffled through the drinks on the wall. In the meantime, Hue stopped pouting after seeing the cue sticks. He wished he had snatched one of them earlier. Maybe then, he could've thrust one through Dabria's chest the moment she introduced herself. He grinned as he walked toward them. While Sofia spent her time rummaging through bottles of whiskey and Heather played with Charlie, Hue wasted no time to make another weapon. He raised one of the sticks high above his head before breaking the upper fourth off with a knee strike.

He brought it to his eye, admiring the sharpness of it.

"Hue!" Sofia called him over. He walked behind the bar, proudly holding his new weapon. "There's something behind these drinks."

Sofia pointed to a red rectangular object hidden between two glass bottles. Hue pushed everything aside and pulled it out. Upon further inspection, they realized it was a small journal with the familiar raven covering the leather cover.

"I didn't see this earlier. Who do you think wrote it? One of Dabria's loyal followers?" Hue asked. He set his weapon down in front of him. He leaned against the wall. "I wonder if it's just a bunch of ramblings."

"We won't know until we read it," Sofia said, urging Hue to open it. Hue flipped to the first page. He let Sofia lean in so they could read together.

"This was back in 1999." Sofia ran her finger under the date.

"Look." Hue moved his thumb to a block of text underneath a scribbled drawing of the hotel.

Today is the day. The day we make the sacrifice to fulfill Dabria's vision. A vision to create a better world by damning every sinner. We have the child we need for it. Her mother was easy to convince. It's a shame such a young girl had to be cast for the role, but the fact that she doesn't have a father means there's one less person to worry about. This bastard child will be the catalyst to set everything in place.

Sofia's eyes ran down to the bottom of the page.

"Go to the next entry," she said. Even though she spoke harshly, Hue didn't mind. His curiosity grew as strong as hers. The handwriting on this page suggests the writer's hand was shaking.

The ritual turned into a mess. We chained the girl to a metal slab that swung over the open flame emanating from the cauldron, but her mother must've regretted her decision to hand over the girl. After the child's skin turned black and melted off her body, the chains holding her in place broke, sending her burnt corpse spiraling down. Those shackles couldn't have come undone by themselves. I remember them creaking more than usual after her mother left the chamber earlier that day, and because of this, the little girl knocked that cauldron over. The fire spread throughout the hotel. It burned everyone, including Dabria. Even now, as I write this, the flame is spreading throughout the town. It makes no sense. Only the building should burn, so why is the rest of our home being subjected to it? This was not in the plan. Like everyone else, I aided in this ritual. Perhaps we're being punished for our lack of diligence.

The passage ended in a mess. Tiny slits went down the page as though someone dragged their nails across the paper. Even the bottom had small patches of red. Hue rubbed his finger on it. The stains refused to go away. He took a glance at Heather to make sure she was okay. With Charlie keeping her entertained, Hue moved to the next page, before Sofia said anything else.

This fault is my own as much as it is my brothers and sisters. I can't forget the look the child gave me. Her skin may have been black as coal, but there's no mistaking the intensity in her eyes. I don't know why my heart aches. I'm a loyal disciple of Dabria, yet I feel as though she may have been wrong. Perhaps I'm being punished. Perhaps my doing in this ritual is my sin, and Heather is just an innocent child. Sofia's eyes opened wide when she saw Heather's name.

"Hue, what if—" He shushed her. Despite having plenty of questions of his own, he wanted to plan out how he'd tackle the information. Without a doubt, Lisa was hiding something from them, and Heather was at the center of everything.

"We'll ask her," he said, referring to Heather. "We just need to come up with our best approach." Hue placed the journal down on the bar.

"Okay, then. But let me just say some things so we can brainstorm." Sofia placed her hands on the wood and leaned forward, trying to push out the words she wanted to say. "If I remember correctly, the bible Lisa gave me mentions a sacrifice. If Heather is that sacrifice, then how is she even here with us? She's already dead. Just like Lisa. Why would they want to sacrifice her again? To punish her? Or maybe because Dabria and the rest of them don't know they're already dead?" She raised her voice. When Heather turned to them, Hue gave her a fake smile.

"We're almost done here," he told her. Heather went back to playing with Charlie.

"That's probably true. Considering all the things we've seen, I can believe Lisa's words. Heather is a dead girl walking among us, but you know what happens when we travel to this town. The blizzard always takes over, and when that's done, everything changes positions according to where we are. Sofia, we're trapped here. We can't run anymore. If we have to face a bunch of ghosts, then we will." Hue dug his fingernails into the bar. With their worsening crisis, he didn't feel confident in being able to survive.

Sofia retrieved the journal and began flipping through the entries again. "Let's just hope we find something in here. I don't know what, but even a tiny bit of information will help us."

The fire spread all throughout the basement. It devoured the stone floor as though we were in a house made of wood. Not a single surface was immune to the flames. Once that child knocked over the cauldron, our order broke apart. Even Dabria burned as we ran out of the basement. That hotel became our final destination. Before the cowardly few of us broke through the front doors, other men, such as me, repented one last time. After all, that hotel was more sacred than our church. People were only confident enough to leave this town after they went in here to repent.

Sofia began connecting the dots. With Dabria's obsession with repentance and her cult putting all their attention on the hotel, she realized she was thinking about it all wrong. They had to go to the hotel. Not to fight, but to talk, and then they could leave. She looked at Hue. His eyes were glued to Heather. She didn't even realize his attention drifted from the page.

"We have to get to the bottom of this," Sofia said.

Hue sighed. "I guess so." Without saying a word, they understood that the town's history would inevitably make a fatal collision with them. "They'll be at the hotel, waiting for us, won't they?" Hue asked. Sofia gave him a sad smile. "And even if they're not, we both know they want Heather. We can't let them have her." Heather ran her fingers through Charlie's fur. The idea that the cult wanted her didn't sit well with him.

"I'm not leaving," Sofia whispered, as she ground her teeth. Hue nodded in agreement. Sofia started shifting through the pages again, hoping to find more information on Heather.

"Do you think Heather did something bad, just like us?" Hue leaned forward on the bar. His knuckles turned white as he clenched his hand into a tight fist.

"Look." Sofia brought his attention to the window without answering his question. The snow outside was melting.

"Hold on," Hue muttered. He strode toward the front door. After opening the door and peeking his head out, the air formed a strong grip around Sofia's lungs. Hue pulled himself inside.

"Hue!" Sofia yelled at him as he rolled on the floor in a coughing fit. Heather rushed to his side. She inspected his face.

"The snow. It's melting. It feels like summer outside, and the sun is rising." He suppressed a scream. Sofia's mind immediately went back to her readings. The journal and bible became deeply intrusive thoughts.

"It has to do with the fire we read about it. The fire that started in the hotel." She shoved the small journal into her pocket. Sofia spoke with conviction. Figuring out the secrets of Twin Peaks while being hunted by its residents didn't sit well with either of them.

"Well, since we're here to be punished, I don't really think it's fair to Heather." Hue's eyes drifted toward her. Could her sin be the failure of the ritual? If so, Dabria was crazier than they thought. "I don't know why she'd be here."

"I can't think of a reason either," Sofia said, "but it's time we spill everything out. We're going to be facing not just Dabria, but ourselves too. We might as well get ready." Just as soon as Sofia made her proposal, Hue stiffened his shoulders. "You always mention your parents. How bad was your relationship with them?" She dropped a bomb on him. His face turned into a contorted mess as he suppressed a scream.

"You're really going for it, aren't you?" Hue averted his gaze. "I'll tell you, but you have to be open to me as well."

"Of course." Sofia nodded. She waited for him to speak, but he only did so to lecture her. "I've already told you my story. I have an abusive stepdad, and I almost killed him." He paused to let his words settle in. "You'll talk about yourself first, and then I'll add a few extra details about myself." Even though a strong surge of anger flowed through him, he felt more in control than before.

***

Sofia racked her brain. Hue was right. She asked him about his mistakes without considering her own. She only knew Dabria brought her in regards to her parents. The memories the cultist brought up during their kidnapping were just proof of that.

"It has to be about my mom." Sofia's voice trailed off.

"And? What else?" Hue pressed forth. But as his footsteps got closer, Sofia felt the need to shrink into the smallest version of herself.

"To be honest, I don't know." Hue sighed. The dissatisfaction with her answer was written all over his face. "I swear, I don't know!"

"I get it. I don't think you're lying. I just think you need to figure out what you did wrong. Otherwise, we're both screwed." Hue turned his attention to the falling ash. "We've been here long enough. Let's just get moving."

Sofia nodded. The disappointment she had in herself grew until it consumed her. Hue went to the bathroom, mumbling something about hoping to find more supplies. Perhaps there'd be cardboard boxes waiting to be discarded. Meanwhile, Sofia went to the bar to loot it for food. She listened to Heather playing with Charlie to ease her mind. But without a bag, she forcefully stuffed every edible-looking thing into one pocket.

"Hue!" Heather screamed. By the sound of it, Hue rummaged through the trash bins and closets. He stopped when Heather called out.

Sofia turned around to see that the girl and Charlie had vanished. She stared at the exact point where they'd just been a moment ago.

Hue ran out of the restroom and scanned the room. Confused, he looked at Sofia. "Where is she?" he yelled. "She just called for me!"

Sofia accidentally dropped the limes in her hands. Charlie's growl, as well as the shattering of windows, resonated outside.

"Sofia!" Heather screamed in the distance. Neither one of them knew the direction, so they opted to burst out of the bar and hope for the best. Hue slammed his body through the wooden door with his new spear in hand.

"Heather!" he called out to her, but this time the noise completely died. Sofia bumped into his back once she ran outside. "I don't hear her." Hue breathed heavily. "What about Charlie? Do you see him?"

Sofia scanned the area in front of them. "No, they're both gone."

"Damn it!" Hue stomped the ground. Sofia felt a slight amount of pain since the frozen air was replaced with a fiery atmosphere.

"I'd bet she's being taken to the hotel. Everyone, even us, has eyes on that place," Sofia said.

Hue nodded. "That's right. There's no time to waste. I just hope that dog is as good as you claim. Maybe we'll be lucky enough to have him help us."

***

Hue looked at the hotel in the distance. He used his hand as a visor to prevent the sunlight from hurting his eyes. He didn't care about himself anymore. After seeing how much people like Dabria and Harry inflicted pain on others, he just wanted to stop them, even if it meant violence. "Let's go." Together, he and Sofia left the bar far behind them. The race to the hotel began.

Chapter 17

Right after leaving the bar, the heat grew in intensity. Not only that, but the pungent smell of burning corpses filled the air. It felt as though Dabria was taunting them. Reminding them of Heather's fate. Sofia tore off a few blank pages from the journal. She and Hue used their shoelaces to tie the paper to their face. The makeshift masks were a horrid abomination, but they didn't have anything else. With the stench assaulting their noses, they knew the whole town would be consumed by it.

"I'd rather have the blizzard," Hue said. They trudged forward through the painfully humid air. Sofia couldn't help but think how low their chances of survival were. Dabria took complete control. They could only play by her rules. With Heather gone, and Lisa transformed into some kind of monster, her heart spiked at the thought of what their fate could be. "Just make sure you don't suffocate." As always, his voice broke through her negative thoughts. Even though Hue spoke in a commanding tone, it still left her feeling protected.

Oddly enough, just like her father, he made sure she walked on the inside of the sidewalk.

"Hue," Sofia said.

"What is it?"

"I'm sorry." He eyed her curiously. She seemed to catch wind of it. "You've done so much already, and I've just been questioning everything." Hue gave a short nod.

"No, that's not true. You've been a great help. If it weren't for you, I'd probably have lost my mind." He kept his eyes forward.

"But—"

"Now isn't the time to doubt yourself," he interrupted. Hue sped up into a light jog. Sofia followed. Their breaths tried to escape their mask, but that only turned the pages into a soggy mess. Sweat beaded down Sofia's chin. Hue felt the same sensation but forced himself to ignore it. Right now, only Sofia and Heather mattered to him.

The little girl kept popping into his thoughts. No matter how hard he tried to suppress the image of her, the intrusive thoughts kept coming. The ash began coming down in droves.

"Tell me if your eyes start to sting. I'll do what I can," Hue muttered.

Sofia looked down. With the gradual sunrise, they could see her shadow. Just as they were getting halfway to the hotel, a big hail of ash shot down from the sky. Hue immediately tackled Sofia to the ground and covered her with his body. It felt like a candle was being held against his back. Sofia flinched as he dug his nails deep into her shoulders—something he couldn't help, because of the pain.

"Hue, please stop," Sofia whispered. But he only hugged her tighter. He was still going about his heroic ways. Hearing the pain in his breathing hurt her. She tried shoving him away, hoping she'd throw him off, and take the ash on her own.

"Don't move." He sensed her intentions, so, she immediately stopped. "Just let this downpour end." It felt like an eternity before he moved, but once he did, he hid the relief that washed over him. "It's over." He helped Sofia up. The first thing Sofia did was stare at him. For a moment, Hue thought she was going to say something, but instead, she slapped him across the face.

"What the hell!" He rubbed his red cheek.

"You're not bulletproof! I can be more than just moral support!" Hue turned to face the road. He ignored her and walked forward. "You don't have to keep putting yourself in harm's way." Sofia jumped in the air and slapped the back of his head. Still, Hue didn't react. A million emotions raced through her eyes.

"Fine," he muttered. He didn't say another word.

Sofia clearly held back her tears. With Heather missing, Hue and Sofia only had each other left. Her body trembled, and both of them became so lost in their own thoughts that they didn't notice the ash stopped falling.

"My mom would say the same thing when it was just us," Hue said in reference to Sofia's outburst. He let out a deep breath as the last piece of ash dissolved into nothing.

"Is there more you want to tell me?" Hue considered her question. Despite Sofia failing to tell him her home life, he figured that he might as well get everything off his chest in case they died.

"There is. And to tell you the truth, you do remind me of her." Sofia's eyes grew wide.

"I don't understand." Hue coughed. He could feel all his sorrows spilling out, but he found it hard to release everything.

"I don't think my mom ever changed. She still loved me even when she met my stepdad. She was just exhausted and scared. The last time we talked, she begged me to leave. She even handed me the keys to our minivan. Even though I almost killed my stepdad, she chose to help me." Sofia said nothing. She looked at him, opening his mouth to say something, but then closing it again. As the silence grew thicker, it seemed to make her more uncomfortable.

"You know, my family wasn't that great either." Sofia kept her words soft. Hue gave her his full attention and remained quiet. "It's true," Sofia continued. "My mom and dad always fought. While my dad endured every bit of verbal abuse from her, in the end, she divorced him. I lost him." The sky's orange tint grew stronger. For the first time, the sky in Twin Peaks became clear. The moon stood next to the sun. "I still remember the day he left. I tried to stop him, but he drove off. Only then did my mom act friendly toward me." Sofia glanced at Hue.

His facial expressions didn't show a reaction. However, internally, he felt the strong urge to hug her. His lips quivered. Words wanted to come out, but by the time that urge hit, he just sunk his tooth deeper into his flesh.

The pain made him cough. He spit out a small sliver of blood. Sofia's eyes locked onto the red liquid. Despite that, she continued her story. "My dad was also an artist. A really good one too. But he gave it up so he could make enough money to satisfy my mom. I called him a 'hero' a few times, but he never liked the title. According to him, 'human being' was more accurate.'"

Hue slowed his pace. He couldn't keep his tooth buried in his tongue anymore. He made eye contact with Sofia.

"How does it feel to have a mom?" he asked. With his head hanging low, Sofia's face dropped. She didn't take into consideration the way he saw his mom.

"I hated her," Sofia said. "She stood between me and my dad. He was the only person that truly mattered to me." She cocked her head to the side. By now, Hue showed vulnerability. The likes of which she had never seen before. Still, she spoke openly. Perhaps sharing their sorrows would do them both some good. After all, Hue's life story would make the thickest book in the world. "So, what about your mom? You seem more conflicted about her than anything else."

Hue sighed. Sweat poured out his forehead, down his cheeks, and dripped off his chin. With the snow gone and the remnants of the ashes scattered around, the air felt warmer. It was as if the town changed seasons within less than an hour. Hue gritted his teeth.

"I'm sorry. I know I wanted to talk about this, but. . . I think I'm done. At least, for now," he muttered.

"Yeah." Sofia's short answer came out as more of a faint breath. They shared a smile. Hue felt a bittersweet feeling in the pit of his stomach. Even though their conversation brought up painful memories, at least he had someone to share it with. Now, he felt a little easier at the prospect of death. But before he could bask in his comfort, Sofia tugged at his arm.

"Look!" She pointed at a bracelet stuck onto the side view mirror of a truck. "That belongs to Heather," she said. Hue's eyes grew wide. The only thing next to them was a giant theater. And unlike the other buildings, this one had its lights on.

"That can't be a coincidence. If they stopped by here, we might be able to get her back before heading to the hotel." Hue sprinted into the cinema before they could discuss a plan. With his broken pool stick in hand, he disappeared through a set of double doors. Sofia snatched the bracelet and rushed in after him. Hue immediately covered his eyes when he set foot inside the massive lobby. The lights were like strong rays of the sun. Not only that but the heater was definitely turned on.

"Why is this place so active?" Sofia asked.

"I don't know, and I don't care." Hue started at the door to one of the rooms. It had been left slightly open. He walked toward it. Instinctively, Sofia waited behind him, ready to support him. If anyone were to jump out, they'd pounce on them without a second thought. Hue kicked open the door. He ran in like a soldier breaching a room. But they saw no one. The screen only played static, accompanied by white noise. Hue beckoned Sofia to stay glued to his back as they checked every aisle.

"I found another one," Sofia said as she lifted another bracelet.

'They were definitely here," Hue muttered.

"Then let's keep searching." He doubted they were still sticking around, but a faint glimmer of hope remained. Hue thoroughly searched every seat. He looked under them for Heather and inside the cup holders for any remnants of her belongings, but as they searched the aisles, the closer they got to the screen, the more it flickered. Until it eventually showed a film. The images on it were colorless and grainy. But without a doubt, the boy shown on screen shared the same features as Hue.

"Is that you?" Sofia asked.

Hue turned his head toward the screen before pulling his gaze back. He looked around for something else to focus on. "My mom gave me a chance to escape. I left my old life behind, and I intend to keep it that way." He walked to the back of the room.

"Hey! Where are you going?" Sofia called out to him.

"I'm going to search the other rooms. You can finish up here." Hue shoved his shoulder through the door. But instead of going into a different screening, he laid his back against the wall. Splitting up was a horrible idea, but he could feel himself on the verge of tears. Seeing his past would hurt him dearly, but at least Sofia could watch it on the big screen rather than having to tell her himself. He listened carefully for any sounds, in case Sofia ran into some trouble.

***

In the meantime, Sofia couldn't help but feel curious. Without Hue there, she was free to watch the film. She stared at the screen.

The projection showed Hue frantically running over wooden floorboards. He crossed a kitchen, dirty dishes dangerously stacked on the counter, then maneuvered around a drying rack in the middle of the living room, until he reached a hall.

His house, Sofia realized.

With heavy breaths, Hue rushed up the stairs. A man who must be Harry, who looked nothing like Hue, followed in pursuit.

"Get over here!" he yelled at his stepson. But Hue only stood at the top of the steps, paralyzed with fear. "Don't even try to run." Harry's heavy footsteps stomped up the wooden staircase. Parts of it cracked underneath his feet. By the time he reached Hue, his fist grabbed onto the fabric of his shirt. Creases formed across his top. Hue grunted before being shoved into the wall behind him. The back of his clothes turned into a light blue.

The wall behind him looked like it had been recently painted.

"Get away from me!" Hue threw a kick that sent Harry flying back. His bones cracked as his body struck every step on the way down. Even though his eyeballs moved, the rest of his body remained motionless. "No, please." Hue tripped down the stairs as he tried to get to him. He landed on Harry with a loud thud. Hue held his hand over the man's mouth to make sure he could feel his breath. His mom rounded the corner. Hue stopped and stared at her. "Mom?" His voice wavered. He brought his

arms up to protect himself. She never laid a hand on him, but after being Harry's punching bag for so long, he came to expect it.

She knelt, caressing Harry's head. Harry's eyes moved to her as she ran her fingers through his hair.

"Mom, I didn't mean to." Hue fell to his knees, crying profusely, but instead of being angry, his mom pulled him in for a hug. He wrapped his arms around her. "Mom, why did you choose him over me?" She squeezed him tighter into her chest. "You had a choice." He gritted his teeth. "Why didn't you choose me?" Hue gave a loud shriek as he cried into her shoulder. "If it weren't for you, we wouldn't be here! This wouldn't have happened! So why didn't you choose me?" His voice tore at the strength of his cries.

"Hue, please. You have to leave before it's too late." She let go of him. He stared at her, dumbfounded. It had been years since she spoke to him directly. "Here." She tossed him a set of keys. "Drive, and don't come back." Her voice came out as a whimper. "Drive down the road. It'll take you straight to Des Moines. At least there, you can hide with your aunt." Hue's mouth fell open. Gratitude glittered in his eyes.

"Mom, why can't you come with me? I don't have to hide in Des Moines. It'll be just the two of us. Like it should have been." She yanked him to her chest. Her soft fingers ran through his curly hair.

"I'm sorry." She shushed him while gently rocking him. "You should know that I always loved you." Then, without giving him closure, she pushed him back, shoving the car keys against his chest. He gave a short nod, stood, and sprinted for the minivan outside.

As Hue's life faded from the big screen, Sofia's mind replayed bits of it in her head. Hearing someone tell their story didn't have the same effect as witnessing it.

That's why he's here? For permanently crippling his stepfather?

"Sofia!" Hue yelled from the lobby. She didn't have time to con-template. Her legs carried her out the exit as fast as possible. Her blood pumped through her but only burst through her veins when she swung the doors open. A monster stood on top of Hue. He writhed on the ground, punching with his right hand and pushing its mouth away with his left. Unlike the first monsters they encountered. This one looked more human, just like Lisa. Hue reached for his spear that he dropped to his side, but that brief second of distraction cost him two of his fingers.

The thing cut off his pinky and ring finger with its razor-sharp teeth. Hue screamed. "Sofia!"

She ran forward, screeching and hopping on the monster's back. She put all her strength into pulling it away, but the moment the monster turned to look into her eyes, she froze.

"You little bastard," Hue muttered to the creature. With its atten-tion focused on Sofia, Hue managed to reach his spear and used the opportunity to stab through its skull. As soon as it died, Sofia rolled to the ground. His bloody teeth landed on Hue's shoulder. He grunted as he pushed away the corpse. "Thanks."

"Hue, your hand." She inspected the nubs of where his fingers used to be. She tore off a piece of her shirt to bandage his wounds.

"These things are starting to look more human," Hue said, ignoring the pain. His hand stung, and the crude bandage didn't help much. Rather than answering, Sofia maintained her focus on patching his broken body. Afterward, Hue poked at the body with his stick. "It's definitely dead." The hole went from under its chin and straight through the top of his head. Unlike his other kills, he came to a resting heart rate within a couple of seconds. He became used to the brutality of Twin Peaks. He knew he'd have no problem killing everyone else that came their way.

"Hue, I want to talk about you," Sofia said in a soft voice.

He eyed her suspiciously. "What?"

She fidgeted with the rim of her shirt as she spoke. "I saw what happened between you and Harry. I saw it in the theater." Sofia bowed her head. She seemed ashamed for her bluntness, but he gritted his teeth. He never intended for her to see the monster he turned into. His violent past haunted him. But after their recent scuffle, he couldn't act innocent.

"Now, you know who I really am. I just wish I knew everything about you." His voice quickly went silent. With a frown on his face, he knelt to examine the monster's face. A morbid sense of curiosity took hold of him.

"I told you everything. I still don't know what Dabria wants from me." He didn't respond. He tapped his fingertips on the jagged ends of the corpse's teeth. "Hue, I know I haven't been as open as you are, but please. Just bear with me." Hue let out a sigh. He stood and walked past her. The silence he gave her struck her heartstrings harder than any attack from a monster. Hue wanted to see the film himself. But after stepping back into the cinema, his gaze rested on the aisle closest to the speakers. Right there, a cultist carried an unconscious Heather over his shoulder. Two other men stood by his side. Hue immediately ran after him. Sofia jumped through the doors as soon as she heard his frantic footsteps.

"The boy and the girl!" One of the men pointed at Hue. Despite having the appearance of a wounded dog, Hue didn't fight like one. Instead, he kept the strength of a lion. To him, those men were nothing more than a few obstacles, objects he could use to express his anger. They ran like a stampede of zebras. Sofia lagged behind him. In the end, he followed them through the emergency exit before Sofia could even get halfway through all the rows of seats. As soon as he ran out, one of the men threw black powder in his eyes. Hue thrashed his arms in a blind rage.

The entire world turned dark. He heard them scurrying away. So, he stumbled forward, following the sound of their heavy boots.

***

In the meantime, Sofia finally reached the speakers at the very front of the theater, but just as she turned on the balls of her feet, a hand reached out. A piece of cloth was shoved in her mouth. She threw her skeletal arms in a frenzy. Hue was just outside, but she wasn't sure if he could see her. Sofia's dampened screams turned silent. The man shoved her into a chair. Her leg shot out, sending a kick to his groin. The strike forced him to stumble away.

She jumped on her feet. Her throat tensed, ready to yell for help. But the man propels himself at her. Again, he goes for her mouth. He shoves the cloth deeper into the edge of her throat, making her gag.

"This will only take a moment." He held her down, and she squeezed her eyes shut at the sight of his dagger. "I don't care about your repentance. Trying to save the girl is enough to warrant death." At that moment, she summoned her happiest memory as a form of comfort.

She ran around the park with her dad chasing her. He moved just as fast as the wind. Her gleeful screams and dinosaur-like roars flew around the playground. That happiness persisted until she tripped. Instead of her shorts taking on the grass, they flew upward, forcing her knee to take the injury.

"You have to be careful." Her dad laughed as he inspected her knee. *Despite the pain, Sofia smiled at her father's generosity. "It's always good to play."*

Her mother scowled. "Sofia! It's time to eat!" she called out. Her mom sat at a picnic table. An assortment of food waited for them.

"Not yet!" Sofia replied. She jumped on her feet, stretched her arms out, and ran around the field. She hadn't eaten since last night, not as a form of punishment, but because she chose not to. She favored playing with her dad non-stop. Her mom always scolded them for it. Saying that he needed to be more responsible. But Sofia only cared about having fun. The type of fun her dad provided her. However, the further she ran, the quieter it became. After turning her head, she noticed her dad didn't chase after her. She stopped in her tracks. Almost scraping her skin against the grass.

She saw her mom yelling at her father. Their bickering started to get the better of them. Even though another couple witnessed them throwing insults back at each other, this time, they didn't even care. Usually, these fights were contained within the privacy of their house, but not now. Her mother just looked so fed up.

"She only likes you because you're the 'fun' parent!" her mom yelled. "Without me, she'd be a mess. Just because I value responsibility doesn't mean I'm a terrible person! When that girl grows up, she's going to need me more than ever!" She marched toward her daughter. Sofia tilted her body to look past her mom. Her dad stood still. Staring at the ground. "Such a horrible role model," her mom muttered.

***

Hue finally managed to clear his vision. The dark substance still covered his hands, but the burning sensation on his face disappeared. With no one else in front of him, his shoulders slumped. He failed. They took Heather. He clenched his fist, trying to suppress the rage growing within him.

I'll get them. He knelt to inspect their tracks. The soles of their boots deeply embedded themselves into the leftover ash. He slowly looked in front of him. They led deep into the trees away from the main road. He let out a deep breath. Just then, he heard Sofia's muffled scream. He turned around and slammed his shoulder through the door.

"Sofia!" At first, he didn't see her, but when the cultist's blood-soaked dagger glimmered in the light, Hue sprinted in their direction. By the time he reached her, the man was ready to bring his weapon down. Without hesitation, Hue took him down. Sofia's hand throbbed. Hue lost two of his fingers, but she had a hole in her palm. While she stood up in a daze, he wrestled with the man. The guy's brown robes ruffled against the chairs. This time, Hue's moves seemed more technical, as though he had trained in martial arts for years. "Stop struggling!" Hue's words rang out, but she didn't register them. She only saw their blurry figures in a heated scuffle. But after Hue threw him onto the chair, he pressed him into the cushion by forcing his foot into his chest.

Considering that he lost his hand-crafted spear, he didn't put himself in a desirable match-up. Out of the corner of his eye, he saw the blood trickling down Sofia's fingers. He wanted to yell at her, but in her dazed state, he didn't know how long it'd be until she recovered. For him, losing his fingers momentarily put him in the same state. But he knew they were very different on the inside.

Eventually, Sofia came to her senses. After the pain became unbearable, she looked to Hue for comfort. However, after seeing him in the middle of an interrogation, her demeanor changed. He yelled at the cultist, demanding information about Dabria.

"What are you asking him?" she asked, stopping next to Hue. Their captive eyed Sofia.

"If you move toward her, I'll take you down again." Hue didn't hesitate to conjure another threat. The man tossed his dagger on the ground and put his hands in the air. Hue smirked at him. "Since your friends are long gone, how about you help us get Heather back? Maybe we could trade you for her."

The man laughed at Hue's suggestion. "They don't care about me. I don't even value myself. As long as we finish the sacrifice, we can change the world." Sofia spat at his face. She pushed Hue to the side to start her own interrogation. At that moment, Hue feared her more than anything else. She never snapped at someone like that, and he never expected her to.

Sofia slapped him across the face. Her blood smeared his gas mask. Her hand became numb. The damage had been done, but for now, she couldn't feel it. In fact, she couldn't even feel her left arm at all. She wanted to tear his mask off. Seeing that black smoke escape his lungs would've put a smile on her face. She gritted her teeth.

"It's okay," Hue whispered to her in a soft tone. He could tell she was starting to slip into the same violence that consumed him. "Just focus on patching your hand." Sofia's glare softened when she saw his hurt face.

"I'm not making a request," Hue said to the man. "We need Heather, and you're going to help us get her back." He scoffed at Hue.

"That won't happen. We'll—" He stopped his sentence short when Hue grabbed the filter of his mask. "I can take you out of this world at any moment." Hue taunted him. The cultist gave his toughest act.

"I already told you; I don't care about myself. I just care about the future of this world." Hue sighed.

"I'll just make you talk," he muttered. Hue looked to Sofia. "I'm sorry you're caught in all of this," he whispered. Her eyes popped.

"Hue. . ." As he raised his fist in the air, the man kicked him in the groin. Hue grunted. He fell on his bottom, fearing he would go after Sofia next.

"You're not getting anything out of me." Much to their surprise, he undid the straps of his mask and yanked it off. Just as expected, the black smoke escaped his lungs and dissipated into the air. His body slumped in his seat.

Chapter 18

Hue narrows his eyes at the man's corpse. His robes sunk deeper into the chair as his body turned into black liquid. Hue quickly rummaged his hands through the folds of his robe.

"What are you doing?" Sofia asked. Her voice trembled, still shaken by the cultist's willingness to die for their absurd cause.

Hue beckoned her to come closer and gave a short nod at what was left. Sofia picked up the deflated pants. She shook them vigorously until the faint sound of fabric grinding against each other caught her ears.

"Hue," she said.

"What?" He let go of the robes to face her. "These fell out of his pockets."

She showed him two Polaroid photos of teens she didn't recognize.

Hue came closer, and together, they inspected each picture. The first one was of a boy who seemed slightly younger than both of them. He was short with a lanky build, and judging by the hospital gown and tear-stained eyes, he didn't seem to be well off mentally. When

Sofia turned the picture around, the name "Charlie" was written on the back.

"What the hell?" She stabbed her finger at the name. "Hue, do you think that's our Charlie?"

Hue shook his head. "If it is, then I'd be even more confused than when I found myself here."

Sofia eyed the photo a little longer and then pointed at the bottom right-hand corner. "Saved," she read aloud. "Hue, something's off about this. What about everything else that came out of his pants." Before she could even bring her eyes to meet his, Hue was already examining another photograph and the note attached to it.

"Look at this one." Sofia brought her face next to his as they viewed the picture. This time, a teenage girl stood in the forefront of it. She smiled wide with a lit cigarette in her mouth and both her hands, giving the camera her middle finger.

"Well, Ella looks a lot happier than Charlie," Hue said, pointing at the girl's signature in the bottom left corner. Then, they brought their attention to the note.

My loyal followers,

I love every one of you. Therefore, reminding you of your previous mistakes pains me as much as it pains you. Keep the faces of Charlie and Ella in mind. These were two young souls that slipped out of our saving grace at the last moment. They left our town's haven as one of the 'saved,' but chose to hinder us by taking the form of an animal and guiding all the future sinners to stray from our desired path. Do not let this happen once again.

"This just gives us another reason to get to that hotel," Hue said impatiently. He passed the letter to Sofia. Her eyes focused on the information of 'the saved.'

"Charlie," Sofia whispered. "Charlie was definitely a person, just like us."

Hue raised an eyebrow at her. "So?" he asked.

"If Charlie is one of 'the saved,' then he can help us. We just have to follow him, wherever he goes." Hue thought about her words.

"I don't know. He didn't do a good job at keeping Heather with us. And we haven't seen him since." His eyes drifted from the remnants of the man's clothes, then back to Sofia.

"Hue, she's trapping us into a corner. We need whatever help we can get. Even if you don't think Charlie is that useful, anything to save Heather is what we really need."

Hue sighed. "Fine. As long as we can all get out of here, that's all that matters." Hue shuffled toward the main lobby.

"Hold on!" Sofia placed a hand on his shoulder before he even created one foot of distance.

"What is it now?" A hint of annoyance infected his throat. All the senseless violence and resurgence of his past made it harder for him to remain calm.

"Remember when you asked me what my sin was? I think I'm starting to understand it." Hue removed his hand from her shoulder. "The moment I saw that dagger rise above my head, I thought about my dad again. Just to keep me happy, but since I arrived here, all my memories have slowly gotten clearer. I'm starting to think that my dad isn't the man I thought he was." Hue narrowed his eyes. With his foot on the step above her, he looked down at her head. "It's just a feeling," she said, shaking her head.

"You still don't sound too sure." Hue raised an eyebrow.

Sofia's lips quivered. "I just. . . It's hard to see my dad as anything other than a hero."

Hue put a hand on her shoulder when he noticed her trembling hands. "Why don't you try telling me something from your past that stuck out?"

***

Sofia's mind drifted back to her childhood, and she became so lost in telling her story, that she forgot Hue was there.

Sofia's small legs turned to jelly as exhaustion overtook her. Again, she and her dad spent another afternoon in his art studio. To them, it became a private place, especially since her mom hated the sight of it.

"Daddy?" Sofia said while she sat on the carpet.

Her dad stopped his paintbrush in the middle of his stroke, and after he pulled away from the canvas, Sofia giggled at his blue-stained cheeks. "What is it?"

"Why doesn't mom ever play with us?" Her dad brought his face back to his painting without saying anything. "She's working. She always is."

"But why doesn't she join us when she isn't working?" Sofia's voice rose in pitch before she lay on her back.

"She's just tired from work." Sofia stared at the ceiling, blowing bubbles with her saliva. Earlier that evening, the ceiling fan stopped working. Every sliver of paint started to melt. At first, her father screamed at the sight of it, but again, he found a way to turn that disaster into another piece of art.

"Why don't you work?" Sofia asked. She jumped on her feet, ready to play again. Her mouth opened wide, revealing her missing front teeth, but her dad didn't share her excitement. Instead, he looked down on her. His eyes seemed like empty sockets devoid of emotion.

"I am working," he said in a deep voice. "Right now, I'm painting, and yesterday, I was drawing. This is my job." Sofia looked at him in bewilderment. Her mind couldn't comprehend what her dad was saying. Her mom always emphasized that working led to a paycheck, and that paycheck led to money they could spend, but her dad's art didn't do any of that.

"But Mom said you're not working because you're not earning anything," Sofia retorted. She didn't mean to speak in a snarky tone, but after hearing her mother speak with that tone of voice so frequently, Sofia's speech became similar when she regurgitated her words.

"Sofia, why don't you just go back to enjoying yourself? I saw you drawing in that notebook I bought you." Her dad's face contorted from an angry expression, then back to a neutral one.

"But Mom said—"

"Enough!" For the first time in her life, her dad raised his voice at her. Her tiny heart began pounding out of her chest, and tears welled up in her eyes.

"I'm sorry, Daddy." Her voice broke apart as she tried to contain herself. "Please, don't be mad." Finally, her tears poured out of her face.

"It's okay. I should be the one to say sorry." He put his brush down and hugged Sofia. "Let's go play another game." He shushed her while patting her back.

Sofia stood still. She didn't want to stop seeing her dad as the heroic being he always was, but then again, self-reflection was inevitable.

***

Sensing the riot brewing in her mind, Hue didn't press for more details. "You can tell me more on our way out," Hue said. He took

Sofia's hand and tugged it. She stumbled forward, obviously lost in some kind of internal war. So, instead of standing, he took the time to cut off a piece of the man's robe. With the dagger in hand, she managed to take a long stretch of cloth. For a moment, he stared at the shiny blade that once stabbed through Sofia's hand. Hue only saw himself using it for another senseless murder. Therefore, he dropped it on the floor.

"Dad. . . Mom. . ." Sofia muttered under her breath. Hue ignored her ramblings, choosing to carefully bandage her hand. Blood soaked through the wraps. The sight tugged at his heartstrings. He knew that the mental torment she entered hurt more than any bodily harm. Hue imagined himself in her position. He knew how it felt to struggle with the inner turmoil he had with his mother. He didn't know how to feel about his mom just as Sofia does with her dad. He tapped her shoulder.

"Let's leave," he said gently. This time, Sofia's eyes popped open. Hue sighed in relief. They had to go, so taking a gamble on whether she'd snap out of her trance felt great when it paid off.

"Yes." Sofia nodded as she said it. Hue led them outside. Sofia's hand cramped up as soon as the wind blew through her bandages. Hue sucked in the air when he felt the rising heat. He plunged his hand deep into his pockets, hoping to avoid a burning sensation on the stubs of where his fingers used to be.

"Let's get there before everything collapses." They left the theater behind. Sofia looked back at the monster they had slain in the lobby.

"Hue," Sofia whispered.

"What?" He turned around, taking in what he saw. Just like everything else, he hoped the monster would become a distant memory. Sofia caught up to him and followed him with a gentle smile.

"Thank you for your help." He became enamored by the sight of the orange sky shining on her head. Despite the warm sky originating from a violent fire, she looked beautiful. He made a brief comparison of her and his mother. The way her hair shined reminded him of their morning walks. Perhaps Sofia's resemblance to his mother was why he felt so protective.

"You're welcome," Hue said in a gruff voice.

***

Sofia smiled at the back of his head. And when she looked down at her wrapped hand, her smile grew even wider. She still saw him as an odd character, but at the very least, he did his best to care for her like her dad did and took responsibility as her mom did. She brought her mind back to her parents. Seeing her parents as equals never occurred to her. Still, she couldn't help but see her mom in a better light. She counted all the things her mom did and her dad didn't do. First, her mom kept a job to keep the family afloat, and she made sure Sofia went to therapy. Of course, Dr. Hoffman didn't suit her, but she knew what her mother's intentions were. At the same time, she wished she showed the same amount of compassion as her father.

***

"Hue," Sofia said softly, but he didn't answer. Instead, he kept leading her on a straight path. Despite accepting the harsh realities of his crimes, he knew that leaving wouldn't be easy. He knew Harry almost died because of him, but Hue wanted to believe he could make up for it by saving the lives of Heather and Sofia. They deserved to live.

He heard Sofia saying his name but chose to ignore it. In the end, he decided that whatever happened in the hotel, no matter what it took, he would save the girls. No matter what. "Hue, what's wrong?" Sofia spoke louder.

"Oh, I was just thinking about what to do once we get out of here."

"What?" Even though she registered his words, the sudden optimism seemed to catch her off guard.

"Yeah, what do you think you'll do once you get out? Do you think you'll look for me?" Sofia bit down on her lower lip.

"Definitely. I'll fly out to Des Moines if I have to." She watched Hue's reaction carefully. He bowed his head in shame. Sofia tightened her fist.

"Do you think you'll see your dad again?" Hue wanted to take her mind off their inevitable confrontation with Dabria. Not only that, but he hoped that making her optimistic about her own future would ease the blow if things went awry.

"Hue, what's wrong?" Sofia cut straight to the point.

"Nothing." He shook his head. But upon doing so, she grabbed his arm and came to an abrupt halt.

"No. I don't know what's going through your head, but we're here to work together."

"Like I said, there's—"

"Listen to me!" Sofia raised her voice. "I already told you that you don't need to take everything on all by yourself. We're a team." Hue frowned. No matter how much he wanted to express himself, he never felt comfortable opening up to anyone. And even if he did, he had a hard time putting his feelings into words.

"Okay then." He grunted. "I just want to make sure you and Heather get out of here. I honestly don't care that much about myself." Hue spoke so fast that he became winded. "So, no matter what happens, at the very least, just do your best to stay out of trouble." He took a deep breath.

***

Sofia's eyes turned wide at his confession. Her hand turned into an open palm. She didn't care how much her wound would hurt; she wanted to smack him senseless until he saw just how wrong he was.

"Like I said, we're a team. We'll get out of here together," she said, and then she let out a sigh. Seeing him willing to throw himself in the line of fire bothered her just as much as Heather's circumstances.

Before their argument could further escalate, Charlie came out from one of the cars parked by the sidewalk.

"Charlie," Hue said quietly. The dog ran up to Sofia and rubbed his face against her leg.

"Hi," she said. She instinctively petted his head, more to comfort herself than Charlie. "You were a lost kid, just like us. What brought you here? Who is Ella?"

Charlie took a step back. If he truly lived as a human before, then he definitely became a 'saved' to help people like them. Sofia ran her fingers over the top of his head, and just like any other dog, he reveled in it. His eyes drifted open and shut. Meanwhile, Hue slowly made his way toward them.

"It's you again." Unlike Sofia, he didn't kneel to pet him. Instead, he stood tall, towering over him. "I need you to help us rescue Heather." His voice held the same firmness it had before, except this time, his rage vanished. Charlie retreated from Sofia's arms to sit in front of Hue. The dog looked up at him and barked. "I guess he understands me," he said to Sofia. Charlie looked at him. He stood on his legs and raised his paw down the road. Hue made eye contact with him. Charlie sniffed the ground as they walked. But eventually, he came to a halt. His nose pointed in the direction of an alley. He pulled his head back and howled with all his might.

Goosebumps rose all over Sofia's skin.

***

Hue peered into the narrow path. A sharp pain stung the back of his head. As he stared into the darkness, his body felt drawn to it. Charlie's howl lowered in pitch until it turned into a growl.

Hue, can't you please get along with your stepdad? He's part of the family now. His mother's voice echoed in his head. She held the same somber tone on the day he ran away. Hue ground his teeth together. First, the town taunted him with reminders of his past, and now they were throwing a decisive blow to his mental health.

***

In the meantime, Sofia felt the distressing presence of her own mother. Just like Hue, the dark alleyway called to her. But she didn't hear any voices. Instead, she only felt pressure being applied to her throat. Almost as if invisible hands were wrapping their fingers around her neck. Her vocal cords tightened, preventing her from screaming. The air around her grew heavy.

***

"Hey!" Hue said, grabbing her arm. Even though the muffled whispers of his mom still tormented him, he fought through the pain for Sofia. The blank stare on her face told him all he needed to know. "Sofia!" He squeezed her in a death grip.

"Dad?" she whispered. Hue sighed. He looked back at the alley.

"It's not him," he said to Sofia. "I heard my mom speaking to me. Dabria is just trying to break us for good." Charlie sat in front of her, nuzzling his snout against her palm. However, she couldn't escape her trance. "It's time to leave." Hue kept the calmest voice he could.

"Over there," Sofia muttered. "I heard my mom. I heard my dad." She slowly raised her finger toward the darkness.

"I know. I heard my mom talking to me as well." He took hold of Sofia's hand. This time, he didn't have to gain her attention. They trailed behind Charlie, both of them slowed by the voices of their moms.

"Hue?" Sofia asked. It took a moment for Hue to respond. Sofia's voice almost faded into the background. His mother's voice took center stage.

Hubert! Please, get along with Harry. I love you, but even I need to be loved. I feel so lonely without someone to take care of me. As always, his mom's voice spoke loudly, but with a soft inflection. Like a professional trumpet player at mezzo forte.

"Hue!" Sofia yelled his name louder.

"What is it?" He snapped his head toward her.

"That video of your life. The one played in the theater. Do you think you can ever come back from that?"

Hue sighed. "I hope I will. Let's just get to that hotel first. We're getting closer." He looked to the sky. The tall towers grew as they closed the distance. The further they went, the more desolate the world became. Unlike the other streets, they didn't pass any cars. Only a lonely tricycle lay on the sidewalk. The heat turned into a bitter freeze, and with the sun setting, the moon took center stage. Its blue rays put a spotlight on the double doors.

"Is that it?" Sofia asked. The entrance waited for them. After all this time, they finally reached their destination. "I. . ." Sofia frantically looked around. Their entire plan revolved around infiltrating the building, but everything seemed so much easier in theory. Now, they actually had to do it.

"Are you scared?" Hue nudged her with his shoulder.

"I-I. . ." Sofia's voice trailed off. Hue put his hand on her shoulder.

"After we leave, everything can go back to normal." Sofia eyed him. He acted confidently, but fear slowly crept in. Charlie scratched his nails against the metal doors.

Hue nodded. "Even he wants us to go."

Before Sofia could discuss a plan to sneak in, Hue ran forward. He placed one hand on each door and used all his strength to push them open. As he did so, he felt a strong force fighting back. He bit hard on his tongue at the sudden and unexpected resistance. But once he made an opening, he beckoned for Sofia to follow him. Once they were inside, the musty smell of old wood infected their nostrils. Sofia wafted the air in front of her.

"Now what?" Sofia muttered. She steadied her shaking hands and sat down on the couch in the lobby. Her chest rose and fell with each deep breath she took.

"I'll be back," Hue said. Seeing as how they were about to face Dabria at any moment, Hue decided to let Sofia calm herself. He wasted no time at all, to search their surroundings. He walked over to the service desk, wandering past the intense heat that emanated from the other end of the room. Charlie jumped onto one of the leather chairs. He curled up into a ball and rested his head.

In the meantime, Hue rummaged through every drawer behind the desk. Rows of storage compartments dominated the walls. Newspapers and envelopes filled every space. The sweat dripping off Hue's fingertips smeared the ink on every piece of paper. On the other hand, Sofia sweated from the heat rather than anxiety. She took off every extra layer of clothing.

"I got something we could use." Hue tore a map off the wall. He smacked it down on the desk while opening a drawer full of keys. The door across from him had to be hiding more than just heat. Hue locked eyes on the knob, imagining if a massive fire was stirring behind it. The same fire that would char Heather.

"You could've just walked over to me," she said. But Hue didn't respond. Instead, he took the entire compartment.

"How are we supposed to know which key is which?" Sofia looked down at what he managed to retrieve.

"We won't. We'll go through every single one if we have to." Sofia scoffed. Again, they were put at a disadvantage. They'd be lucky to find the right key at the proper time.

"How about you find that key to the room over there?" She pointed to the door where the heat resided behind. Hue wanted to get Charlie's attention first, hoping that he'd continue to guide them. But they quickly realized he vanished.

"Charlie." She did her best to remain composed. They knew that Dabria tried to burn Heather alive, so the heat didn't put them at ease. Hue strode across the room. They huddled behind the door.

Hue examined the handle. "There's no lock," he said with a grin.

There'd be no need to rummage through the drawer at all. Hue instantly gripped the knob. Once opened, a metal staircase going downward greeted them. The orange light from a fire flickered around the steel pipes covering the walls. Hue led the way, taking slow, methodical steps down. After he got halfway across the stairs, Sofia followed. When he finally reached the floor, his feet tapped the smooth stone beneath them. He held his breath as soon as he realized they walked into a den of horrors.

The pipes came in varying sizes, from wide and short to narrow and long. Nonetheless, they did nothing but cover the room with steam. However, the giant hole sheltering the hungry flame became the main attraction. And worst of all, a man leaning against one of the pipes held Heather in his arms. Her soft face looked serene as her cheeks buried themselves into the man's robe. Hue glanced at her. Sofia's finger pressed against her lips. She tip-toed down the stairs, making sure to be as silent as a cat. She carefully placed one foot in front of the other, but Sofia's wounded palm burned itself on the metal railing. She lost her balance and fell forward, smacking her arms on the rail as she tried to regain control.

Hue couldn't catch her before she hit another boiling hot pipe. Even though Sofia muffled her screams, the racket rattled the room enough for the cultist to catch wind of them. Heather's body rolled out of the fog, followed by the man breaking into a sprint.

"Hue!" He didn't need Sofia's warning. He dashed headfirst into the fray. With the decisiveness of a bull, he took control. Hue spread his arms out, ready to tackle the man, but his eyes grew wide when their attacker ducked and used his leverage to decimate Hue's balance. He toppled to the ground. Hue swung back, but only hit the air. After the man slapped the nubs of Hue's missing fingers, the boy screamed.

"Get off me!" He flailed his elbows around, hoping for a lucky strike. Just then, Sofia went in and hopped on the man's back. Her fingers clawed at the goggles of his mask.

"Help me!" She screamed at Hue. He gritted his teeth. With their combined strength, Sofia restrained the man long enough for Hue to tear off his mask. Black smoke flew out of his lungs almost instantly. And just as it faded away, they were back on their feet.

"We have to go. Now!" Hue said.

Sofia lifted Heather's torso. Sweat from the heat and Heather's weight blotched her forehead.

"Let me carry her," Hue yelled. He brushed Sofia aside and scooped Heather like she weighed no more than a feather. "Come on!" He moved faster than ever. He felt like his heart pumped out more than just blood. He jogged faster than Sofia toward the staircase. The light of the lobby turned into a spitting image of heaven, but that light gradually grew dimmer until it went away.

"The girl stays here!" Dabria yelled from atop the stairs. Her voice echoed through the room. She gracefully placed her foot on the cement floor as a few robed men took formation around her. This time, she presented herself more elegantly. She obviously had her dress ironed to perfection. Every piece of fabric went down straight as a pencil. "Stay where you are!" She shot her arms out. An unnerving smile spread across her face. "Sofia, darling, I was wondering when I'd see you again." She stepped forward, while Sofia stepped back. "There's no need to be scared. I know all that goes on. You've realized your sins, haven't you?" She slowly shuffled forward, ready to hug Sofia the moment she could.

"Back off," Hue said, standing in between them. He gently passed Heather to Sofia. "Just let them go." He grumbled. Dabria's expression turned to disgust.

"You brat!" she cussed at him. Hue returned fire by spitting in her face. His saliva drove right into her pupil. She yelped. "You're filled with nothing but violence!"

"And you're the one who's trying to kill others based on your corrupted sense of justice!" Hue yelled again before she could lecture him.

"Apprehend him!" At her command, her followers formed a protective shell around her. While a handful of men stayed by Dabria's side, a couple broke rank to detain Hue.

"Look out!" Sofia screamed. She clutched Heather tightly to her chest. The little girl's face twitched slightly. Just like every other fight, this one ended in brutal fashion, except this time, Hue didn't come out on top. He flopped to the ground after one loud whack to his skull.

"Get off," he said in a faltering voice. He tried to keep his eyes open, but they grew heavier with each passing second. Dabria inhaled deeply as though they were walking through a field of scented flowers.

***

Sofia stared for a few seconds at Hue's chest. It still moved up and down. He wasn't dead.

"Now, come here," Dabria said to Sofia. The rest of the men parted like the Red Sea, and Dabria swooped closer to Sofia. As she stepped over Hue's unconscious body, she reached her hand out to touch Heather.

"Leave us alone!" She shoved Dabria back with her shoulder. The woman gasped. Sofia raised her heel to kick her down, but one of the men quickly restrained her. He snatched Heather while the other one forced Sofia to kneel. "Stop!" She bit the man's finger hard enough to draw blood, but he didn't react.

"I see you're still tense, but just bear with us," Dabria said. She took slow steps forward while everyone else dragged Hue away. "I was just starting to feel proud of you. You're not like that boy. You're kind, and you're capable of change." She ran a finger down Sofia's cheek.

"He's kind, too. Everything he's done. . . He's done for me and Heather." Sofia's breaths came out in short puffs. She felt the moister coming from their proximity. Her chin became drenched in sweat.

"I have a good judge of character." She smiled, but Sofia scoffed.

"If that's true, how didn't you know that one of your followers lost belief in you?" Dabria furrowed her eyebrows. "You're confused, aren't you? I found his journal at the bar. And you act so high and mighty. Yet, you're not the savior you think you are!"

Dabria grunted. "Of course, I encourage love to flourish among my followers. They're like students, after all. But there will always be bad children." She grinned again. Her eyes briefly followed the men who dragged Hue up the stairs.

"They only love you because you took advantage of them. They're damaged kids like me. Kids you lied to when they needed someone!" Sofia stared hard at her. The smile on Dabria's face slowly washed away. Her hands trembled, and Sofia caught the intensity of her long nails.

"Forgive me," Dabria said. "I tend to act out on occasion when we make big changes. I get too excited. It's not the proper image of a leader." She sighed.

"Don't act graceful when you're not," Sofia muttered. Dabria locked eyes with her. In one swift motion, she slashed her nails across Sofia's cheek. The wound she inflicted left four diagonal lines stretching from Sofia's temple down to her chin.

"Let that scar be a reminder to respect your elders." Dabria turned on her heels before walking away. "Lock her in a separate room from the boy and leave the little one here," she said.

"It will be done." They all spoke in a deep voice that tickled Sofia's ears. Her eyes followed the fist above her head. Sofia closed her eyes, waiting to be struck.

"Oh, and more thing!" Once she heard Dabria's voice, her expectations came to a halt. Instead, when she opened her eyes, the man stopped right before his swing. "Make sure you force her to relive her past. Use as many candles and prayers as you need to. They're doing the same with the boy, and I intend it to be done to her as well." Without saying a word, the man nodded. And before she knew it, Sofia fell forward in a daze. The punch to her scalp stung, but the pain slowly faded away, just like everything else.

Chapter 19

Hue awoke from his sleep. In his dreams, he relived his last moments with Harry over and over again. His eyes darted around the room. He lay on a mattress on the floor. Rats scurried across the wood from one hole in the wall to the other. When he inspected himself, his eyes popped wide at the complete lack of restraints. They never failed to bind his body after being captured, so why didn't they do so now? Hue slowly rose. His back popped with each inch.

Where are they? He noticed a lone chair in the corner, beside his mattress. Immediately, Hue broke a leg off. He shifted it in his hands, trying to get a feel for how much it weighed. He gave it a few swings like a baseball bat. Now, he needed to find a way to escape.

First, he tried the obvious. He jiggled the doorknob, but it wouldn't budge. A vent stuck out of the wall. "Crap!" He cursed himself for being short. His body would be able to slide through the shaft like a snake, and if he hadn't broken the chair, he could've used it to elevate himself.

Instead, Hue raised the chair leg. He pushed it into the door like a battering ram. He struck numerous times until his arms gave way, but nothing changed. Everything was still intact. He let out a deep breath. Shame washed over him. He wanted nothing more than to help Heather and Sofia, but he failed.

Even if he did manage to reach them, his strength alone wouldn't be able to get them out.

He thought back to the monsters they came across. Especially Lisa. Her blind rage, combined with her newfound strength, gave her the power to fend off an entire horde of Dabria's followers. Hue slammed his hand against the wall. If only he had that strength. Then, he could get them out. But, of course, facing his own mortality would've been the hardest part. He gritted his teeth. The sound of heavy footsteps pattered through the floor.

"Put the girl in that room." Hue heard the voice of a man speaking. He assumed that by 'girl,' they meant Sofia. After all, he wasn't the one they wanted to get rid of.

"And what of the boy?" the other one asked.

"Leave him be. Dabria is certain that he's fallen into his love for violence."

"But then, why won't he turn? How can she be so sure?" Hue heard a loud smack.

"Don't doubt our lady. Take that strike as a lesson." After that, the footsteps left. Once the echo of their steps disappeared, he leaned his back against the wall.

Dabria was wrong. He hadn't given in to his violent past. But, if she didn't know, then she obviously didn't have eyes on everyone like a god. Hue paced the room. He pondered how he'd beat Dabria.

But after a good ten minutes or so of being confused, he fell on his bottom. He didn't want to give up, but he felt so defeated. However, a knock came to his door.

"Young man, are you in there?" one of Dabria's men said.

Hue jumped to his feet. "Yeah. Why don't you come in and talk?" Hue raised his fist, ready to pounce as soon as the door opened, but instead, he only heard a low-pitched chuckle.

"I'm not coming in there. However, our fair lady would still like to give you one more chance." He slid Dabria's broach beneath the door. Hue's pupils dilated. Despite being a horrid woman, she definitely knew how to look beautiful. And as he stared at the shining piece of jewelry, the man cleared his throat. "Simply pray with the broach in hand, and she'll show you mercy."

Hue shook his head and scoffed. He hated how everyone thought so highly of her. "And what if I don't take this stupid offer?" Hue snarled.

"Then it'd be best to hope our lady is kind enough to deal with you swiftly."

Not too long after that, Hue heard the man's footsteps walk away. He approached the door and retrieved the broach, and as he saw his face in its reflection, Hue let out a single teardrop.

"I'm sorry, Mom," he whispered to himself. After all this time, his hope to see her again remained. Even if it were in a courtroom or through the industrial-grade glass of a prison, that would be enough. He pursed his lips. Lisa's strength, when she turned, was something of God-like proportions. It was the type of strength Hue needed to fight everyone and open a path to freedom for Sofia and Heather.

Do it, Hue thought. Even if it meant making the ultimate sacrifice, he would do anything to save them. Hue raised his foot in the air and crushed the broach. The thunderous stomp sent a small shock wave through the wooden floor, scattering emerald pieces of glass everywhere. He closed his eyes. He felt his heart thumping as he grounded his feet in place. At that moment, he felt a drop of blood roll from his forehead.

Chapter 20

*S*ofia sat on the front porch of her parents' house. Crickets sounded in the garden, and the moon lit the sky. Her little legs swung back and forth over the edge.

"Where is he?" she whispered to herself. Her small hands hoisted her body off the floor. Her dad spent the entire day buying her colored chalk. Her mom insisted on getting proper clothes, but Sofia felt content in an oversized shirt. According to her father, she could wear it as a dress until she grew big enough to use it as a shirt. Sofia smiled at the thought. She traced her fingers over the deer on her shirt. She poked at its nose. "Dad?" she called out to him. But after receiving no response, she proceeded to distract herself again by poking at the deer.

As soon as the moths began circling the lamp above her, her dad stumbled through the grass.

"Hey!" Her dad's deep voice reached her. She squinted her eyes at him. He tripped on his feet, making him smash the beer bottle in his hand. Afterward, he didn't move. He simply blew bubbles with his saliva like a toddler.

"Daddy?" Sofia leaned forward to poke his cheek, and her fingernail nicked his skin.

"Ouch! What was that for?" He looked up at her. Sofia's eyes grew wide. "Mom didn't cut your fingernails?"

Sofia shook her head. "She said it was your turn to do that."

He lay his forehead on the wooden porch and sighed. "I'll do that tomorrow."

"But that's what you said yesterday." Sofia sat beside him. Even though she spoke directly into his ear, he barely seemed to register her voice.

"Are you okay?" Sofia asked. Her voice trembled. Her dad always told her he had fun drinking, and he always enforced the need to have fun.

"Yeah, of course." He burped. He looked past her at the front door, but Sofia just kept her eyes on him until he snickered. A quick shot of spit flew out of his mouth like a bullet. His saliva splattered on the wooden foundation. "Why are you staring at me like that?" he slurred.

Sofia shrugged. "It's almost eleven. Mommy usually wants me to sleep by now, but I'm scared of the dark."

Her dad rolled his eyes. "Now, what shall we do about that? Do you want me to start dancing to scare those monsters away? Maybe I could finally start acting like the clown your mom thinks I am," he grumbled before getting on his feet. His legs shook, ruffling his jeans. Eventually, he made slow movements toward the door. His hips swayed while Sofia held his hand. She giggled at the sight.

"You look funny," she said.

"Yeah, well, your mom doesn't think so." He gripped the handle while Sofia held him.

"Why?" Sofia looked up at him with puppy dog eyes.

"Because she doesn't know how to let loose." He barely managed to shove his key into the lock.

"Here." Sofia reached her fingers forward, and with her help, they entered the house. Immediately, her dad plopped himself onto the recliner, picked up the remote, and played a movie. Sofia sat on the floor beside him.

"How about we watch this one?" The screen stopped on the image of a horror film. The cover showed a woman running around a campground while a masked killer chased her.

"But mom says I'm not old enough for that one cause some scenes show—" Her dad didn't let her finish. Instead, he just pressed play. The introduction started, and Sofia kept her eyes glued to the screen until she passed out.

"Oh, my God!" Sofia jumped at the sound of her mother's screech. She looked at the television, thinking the scream came from the movie. But instead, she only heard grunts and moans. She didn't understand what the characters were doing, but her mom ended the film before Sofia could take another peek.

"Mom, what were those two doing?" Sofia asked. However, instead of prompting an answer, her mother only sighed. She took off one of her shoes and threw it at her dad's chest. As soon as the flat of it hit her dad, he stirred awake.

"What time is it?" he asked in a groggy voice.

"Sofia, leave. I need to have a talk with your father."

"But—" Her mom glared at her. Sofia instinctively jumped back at the sight. She ran outside and shut the door but kept her ear close to it. Inside, she heard her parents argue.

"Look at what you did to her," her dad said sarcastically.

"Don't turn this on me. Yesterday, I told you to buy her some clothes for the start of the school year and put her to bed on time. Now, look what you did! Not only is she still using one of your shirts, but she stayed up all night watching that disgusting film!"

Her mom's footsteps reverberated through the living room. Feeling the tension, Sofia couldn't stand keeping out of the conversation. She held the door slightly ajar to peek in. This time, her mom towered over her father, but as always, he didn't look her in the eye.

"You need to calm down," he said.

"No, I don't! You're still acting so carefree when you can't afford to!" She took off her other shoe and tossed it toward the rack by the closet.

"The kid needs to enjoy her childhood! Can't you see, she won't be young forever! She should enjoy this part of her life while she can." Her dad picked up the remote again and turned on the television.

"I can't believe you. She needs a father, not a playmate. Grow up!" Her mom stormed off. After Sofia heard her mom slam their bedroom door, she stepped in.

"Dad?" She walked in a little shaken, but he gave her a bright smile.

"Everything will be fine. Now, just watch the movie while I make you breakfast." Sofia hopped onto the recliner as soon as he left it, and she quickly settled into the warm cushion he left behind. When she looked at the kitchen, she noticed her dad struggling with a can of beans. He searched through every drawer but never retrieved the can opener. Instead, he opened the pantry and tossed her a handful of Twinkies.

"But Mom doesn't want me to have sugar in the morning," Sofia said.

"It doesn't matter. I'll make a proper meal later." He gave her another smile. Sofia meant to speak up. To remind her father that he didn't make a meal yesterday or the day before. But just as soon as she sat up, he waved her off as if he already knew what she had in mind.

***

Sofia woke in a dull room. Again, she got to take a look into her past. She blinked her eyes a few times until the world became clear. Now, she knew exactly what the dull room contained. It turned out that the soft mattress below her didn't have a bed frame at all, and a lone man kept her company. He stood by the door, holding a leather sack over his shoulder. Sofia rose from the mattress. The tickling sensation of her hair flowing against her face forced a sneeze, and she watched his shoulders stiffen. She backed herself against the wall, expecting the man to abuse her, but he remained stationary.

The complete emptiness of the room exaggerated his appearance. And Sofia felt more tension with him than any other enemy. His posture intimidated her enough to discourage an escape attempt.

"Where's Heather? Where's Hue?" Sofia asked. He shook his head. She saw his eyes blink behind the goggles of his mask. "Can you at least tell me where I am?" He struck the wooden floor with his boot. The room vibrated with the strike. "Please, you don't have to do this. Just let them go." He folded his arms across his chest. "I treated my mom unfairly! She wasn't worse than my dad! I know that now!" Sofia yelled at him. She told him every little memory from her childhood, hoping that her acknowledgment would please Dabria. "There, I know what I've done wrong, and I admit it! Now, go tell Dabria!" Sofia's chest rapidly rose and fell as she tried to catch her breath.

"So, what will you do to repent?" he finally spoke.

"Anything. I'll do anything. Just let me out. Please." He stepped forward.

"Be more specific." He spoke in a low tone.

"If Dabria is so interested in me, how about I serve her in place of my friends?" Sofia batted her eyes at him. She hoped that making a bargain would help.

"No. Their fate is their choice, but you may choose to serve Dabria if you wish." He walked back to the door as Sofia felt tears welling in her eyes.

"No! I want my friends back!" She screamed at him with tears pouring out. "Let me go! Let me out of here!" She finally dismissed the idea of avoiding conflict. Instead, she rushed at him. She lacked the strength Hue had, but she knew her pain tolerance could keep her going, and her adrenaline helped her push her own limits. Before he knew it, she already shoved her shoulder against his chest. He squeezed her wounded hand, forcing a scream. Sofia's throat throbbed at the exertion her voice put it through. She clawed at his mask with her other hand, but before she could rip the mask off, he pinned her against the wall with her wrist pressed into his palms.

Sofia frantically kicked her feet. She smashed her shin against his, but to no avail. Even a strike to the groin didn't make him falter. She stared at the latch on the side of his face—the latch that kept the mask together. She leaned into him with her mouth gaped open, and bit down hard on the leather straps. She pulled her head back as fast as she could. The man screamed through his air filter right before his face became exposed. The black smoke covered Sofia's face, and they both hit the ground.

Sofia coughed up everything that entered her lungs. After the final puffs of smoke escaped, she fell over in exhaustion. Her shoulder hit the man's bag. Pieces of steel poked her skin through the fabric. She let out a sigh.

He had weapons?

She pulled it by the strap. Arming herself would be the best thing to do. However, upon unzipping it, a massive pile of keys greeted her. Unlike the ones Hue took, these had a room number attached by a small tag. Sofia smiled to herself. She didn't have a weapon, but she had a means of escape. She quickly slung it over her shoulder and unlocked the door with the correct key. First, she slowly peeked her head out. No one patrolled either side of the hall. Sofia silently stepped outside and closed her room. And with the red carpet muffling her footsteps, she freely ran wherever she pleased.

Initially, she headed for the stairs, but her ears twitched at the sound of groaning. It came from a room a few doors down.

Hue! She prayed that it really was him rather than another monster.

Chapter 21

Hue bit down on his lower lip until the pain became unbearable. He could feel his body changing the moment he destroyed the broach. He never thought he'd die for a couple of friends he met in a supernatural world. Harry beating him to death had seemed more probable only days ago. But then again, life never went the way he expected. Hue face-planted on the ground. The blood continued down his forehead as drool poured out his mouth. Inside him, he felt his ribs expand. They slowly grew larger, stretching his muscles and skin in the process. Not only that, but he felt his gums receding, and his teeth poked the inside of his mouth like needles.

Then, the hallucinations settled in. Just like when he entered the town, he heard his mother's voice along with childish laughter.

"No. Not yet," he whispered. He couldn't lose his mind. At least not now. He forced himself to fight back the temptation to give in. "I need to kill Dabria. I need to save Heather. I need to save Sofia." Hue slowly pushed himself up into a seated position. Eventually, he managed to get on his knees.

He looked at the door, but it flew open. Sofia walked in.

"Oh my God, Hue." She shoved the key back into the bag. "Hue, what did they do to you?" Once he felt her arms wrapped around his shoulders, he knew she was real.

"Sofia. . . Leave me. Y-you have to."

She receded her hug and looked into his eyes. "Let's go!" She ignored him and put his arm around her shoulder to pick him up.

"Get away from me," he whispered in her ear, but she just kept her mouth shut. The blood completely covered his face. Once it fell off his chin, he threw himself backward.

"Hue! It's not the time to give up!" Sofia rushed to help, but after he let out a loud hiss, she froze. "No, Hue." Her voice trailed off. "We're so close." She reached over to him. But Hue nibbled a bit on her good hand. She flinched and pulled away. Tears escaped her eyes. And once Hue saw her expression, he tried to speak. He wanted to push words out, but his disgusting form prevented him from doing so. Even now, his vision slowly started to fade. "Hue!"

He couldn't see her, but he could hear her. He still retained the rest of his senses. After a few seconds, he could see, but he only saw an outline of her body along with her beating heart. Everything else was black. He didn't see any walls, floors, or ceilings. He simply saw her outline and heart. When Hue snapped his body in a different direction, he saw more outlines in the distance. They were levels below their room.

I can see through everything. He thought to himself. At that point, he went silent. Sofia watched him, hoping this was another nightmare. Hue let the breeze from the ventilation shaft graze his head. And when he figured out its direction, he leaped into the air, shooting himself deep into the wall.

***

After all was done, Sofia sat on the floor, feeling lost. She didn't know why he turned. After all, she knew he had really changed. Nevertheless, that didn't deter her from facing Dabria. If anything, it only fueled her desire to do so. She'd end Dabria's fanatical religion once and for all and save Heather.

Chapter 22

The walk back to the lobby felt like an eternity. Seeing Hue turn into a monster felt like seeing a lifelong friend die. The way he screamed, the expansion of his chest, and the strong leap he made toward the shaft replayed in her head constantly. Sofia swore the hall grew longer with each passing second. Not only that, but her heartbeat took center stage. Just like a musician using a metronome, she used each thump to count the time. After one hundred beats, she reached the staircase leading to the first floor, and after four hundred beats, her big toe touched the lobby. She gently hit the bottom with the weight of a feather. Sofia turned to the door. It opened slightly. Behind it, Sofia heard hushed whispers.

Are they praying again? Sofia heaved a big breath. She only had Heather now. With Lisa gone and Hue finished, she needed to save Heather and get rid of Dabria. At first, Sofia tip-toed, making sure not to make any noise, but the moment she rested her hand on the knob, she burst through like a soldier breaching a room.

"Hello, dear," Dabria said.

Sofia stared her down. The woman stood at the end of the room right next to Heather. The young girl screamed.

"Sofia!" she said. Dabria's men stepped forward, creating a massive wall.

"Hold on." She raised her hand, telling them to be at ease. "Sofia, you look different. I can tell you've changed. Therefore, you have no need to stay. You may return to your world." Sofia tightened her fist. Her shoes pattered on the stone floor as she approached.

"I'm not going to." She gritted her teeth. All the cultists raised their staff in a combat position.

"Hold on!" Dabria said. She stepped aside to fully reveal Heather. They locked her in a metal cage hanging above a fire pit. The little girl swung her tiny prison back and forth. She punched the bars but to no avail.

"Sofia!" she screamed.

But Dabria smacked her metal cage and hissed at the girl. "Be silent!" Heather helplessly stared at Sofia, and she made a non-verbal promise to save her. "Since you're still here, perhaps you'd like to watch. I wouldn't mind welcoming another faithful soul to join our ranks." Dabria's words only stirred disdain in Sofia's heart. To her, the old fanatic had never acted so densely.

"No!" she yelled.

Dabria frowned. She walked past all her men. "Can you repeat that?" she asked politely. She leaned her head forward with her ear pointed out.

"I said, 'no.'" Sofia added more grit to her words. They ground against her teeth like a knife against a block.

"I see. I see." The elderly woman raised her hand only to put it on Sofia's shoulder. "You're still filled with hatred, aren't you? That boy must've infected you with malice." Sofia's eyes grew wide. She didn't want to hear her belittle Hue. Not after what he went through. And not after everything he did for her.

"There's no need to help the girl." Dabria pointed at Heather, who had finally stopped struggling.

Sofia shoved Dabria to the side. Her blue robes fluttered in the air, creating a swift wind that blew past Sofia's skin. Every man who guarded Heather tightened their defenses.

"I had faith in you!" Dabria spit at Sofia's feet. There was no trace left of the graceful demeanor she had before. She bared her teeth at her, and her frenzied movement only gave her a rougher appearance. "You had so much potential. You could have lived a prosperous life!" The heels of her boots clacked the floor. The sound of each step boomed louder in Sofia's ears. "Sofia!" she yelled, but she received no response. Instead, Sofia grabbed the cage. Luckily, no one lit the pit. Otherwise, Heather would have already been melting into mush.

"Get her!" All the men turned to Sofia. But all of them stopped when they heard something crawling in the vents. For once, Dabria held a horrified look. And even though Sofia felt the same horror as she did, she took the chance to free Heather. "Ignore the vent! Grab her!" Dabria pointed at Sofia. Once they all charged, the teen's eyes grew wide. She covered Heather with her entire body.

"Close your eyes," Sofia whispered to her. Rather than being beaten, a horrid creature jumped down from above. It broke through the vent and landed on the man who took the lead. Sofia witnessed his face get torn to shreds. It only took a few seconds, but in those few seconds, Sofia made eye contact with the monster.

It was Hue.

He growled and leaped into the crowd. Everyone thrashed their staff in a frenzy.

"What have you done?" Dabria screamed. She pushed through her men toward Sofia. Seeing the woman move with such speed caught her off guard. Sofia quickly let Heather down.

"I need you to run. You see those stairs over there?" She pointed at the exit. The little girl nodded. "Just leave this room! Keep running, and don't look back." Sofia gave her a slight push before running her shoulder into Dabria. The women wrestled on the ground. Throwing each other in every direction. Unlike Hue, Sofia had never been in a physical fight before coming to Twin Peaks. So, she resorted to pushing and flinging her arms, hoping to get a lucky hit.

She heard Hue's low growl, accompanied by the screams of the men. Whether or not he won the brawl, she didn't know. She just knew that she couldn't let his hard work go to waste. Sofia swung again but missed. Her legs tripped and tangled with each other, making her hit the ground. Then, Dabria seized the moment. She jumped on top of her and began clawing at her face. Sofia screamed at the sensation of her skin peeling off. Hue's voice became lost. His growl ceased, and she only heard the men swinging their weapons.

Hue managed to throw one of them into the pit, but judging by his silence, Sofia knew they lost their surprise advantage.

"Sofia!" Heather called from the top of the stairs. Her voice gave Sofia the strength to keep fighting.

"I already told you to leave!" she yelled as she kicked Dabria off her. Once she got free, she sprinted toward the staircase. On her way there, her face dropped at the sight of Hue being pushed around. He still did more damage compared to his human form, but she knew he'd lose eventually. Even then, the urge to help him surfaced. Beneath that ghastly body was the boy she had met a day earlier. The same boy who gave up his life for them. Hue threw his head back and howled to the sky.

Everyone, including Heather and Sofia, stood still. Dozens of other howls responded to him. Sofia heard paws scratching at the tiny windows near the ceiling.

"They're getting away!" Dabria yelled. She shoved one of the men in Sofia's direction. He stumbled and quickly regained his balance. But that didn't matter. The window on his right side shattered as a husky leaped through. The dog bit down on his arm. He tried to break free, but pretty soon, the building became swarmed with dogs. Every window broke as a handful of the animals broke in.

***

Finally, Hue had room to breathe. Once the men were preoccupied with the dogs, he turned his attention to Dabria. Her eyes widened. With one loud screech, he leaped into the air. Her gaze followed him all the way through until he landed on her shoulders. The weight of his body pushed her to the ground immediately. He couldn't see her, but her outline and heartbeat told him all he needed to know. With that, Sofia covered Heather's eyes as soon as Hue raised his claws. Dabria let out a loud scream that ended in an instant.

***

Sofia turned to the stairs. At the top, Charlie waited. His silver nametag gleamed in the orange light that bathed the room.

"Go!" Sofia commanded Heather. Her stubby legs ran upward, and once she stood side by side with Charlie, Sofia took one last look at the battlefield. Blood covered Hue's hand. She couldn't see Dabria anywhere, but she knew her reign had ended. Hue glanced over his shoulder. Sofia smiled at him, hoping to say her last goodbye. Hue got on his hind legs and charged at her. "I'm so sorry. I wish I could have saved you," she whispered to herself. Hue growled the closer he got. His mind was broken.

So, Sofia raced out of the basement. The last thing she saw was Hue's razor-sharp teeth. With the door locked behind them, Sofia took a moment to breathe. *It's over. It's over.* Charlie ran to the front doors. He sat proudly with his chest out.

"Now what? Do I get to go home? And what about Heather?" Of course, Charlie didn't speak. Sofia scoffed at herself. Even though he lived as an animal, she knew he was a human once. "I guess I'll find out, huh?" Charlie scratched his paw on the door. "Let's go," Sofia said to Heather. The little girl reached for her hand, and the two walked outside.

***

Sofia heard her mother screaming.

"Sofia!" She felt her mother pulling her out of the vehicle. As her jacket rubbed against the top of their upturned car, Sofia's face twitched. She opened her eyes once the snow fell on her cheek. Her mother sat her up and put her hand on her cheek. "Are you okay?" She ran her fingers over Sofia's forehead. Sure enough, there were no injuries. No stab wound in the middle of her hand and no deep cuts on any part of her body.

"Mom," Sofia whimpered. She pulled her mother close to her chest. Her arms wrapped around her tightly as she cried into her shoulder. "I'm so sorry. I'm so sorry."

Her mom retreated from her embrace. She looked at her face. "There's no need to be sorry. It's not your fault we crashed." Her mom patted her shoulder.

"It's n-not that." Sofia's voice wavered. "I'm sorry for the way I treated you. I chose Dad over you even though I had no right to." Her mother gave her a long stare. It was the same expression she'd show whenever she got confused. "Are you mad at me? Because—" But before she could finish, they embraced again.

"I was never mad at you," her mother told her. She ran her hand in circles over her back. "I was just scared that you didn't love me. Everything will be all right." Sofia huddled in the fetal position. Her mother held her like a baby as she cried. But through it all, the sound of a howl in the distance comforted her. Sofia looked to the mountain overseeing the road. At the very top stood Charlie. She smiled at him. Afterward, he raced down the hill, never to be seen again. "I hope that's not a wolf."

Sofia buried her face in her mom's shirt. "It's not. It's probably just a dog."

Her mom stared at her, dumbfounded, but Sofia didn't mind. It was over, and she knew she was safe.

Chapter 23

Luckily for Sofia, none of her injuries from Twin Peaks followed her into her real life. This made the transition back to reality a lot more seamless. Sometimes, it only felt like a distant dream. It had been two weeks since her journey from Twin Peaks ended. By now, she had finished her scrapbook of Hue. She still remembered everything he told her. So, finding out more about him wasn't too difficult. Multiple news sources reported on his disappearance. The moment she saw his face plastered on the internet, she took a screenshot, and she did so on every webpage. Her mom grew increasingly worried at the sight of her printing out a picture of him.

To her, her daughter had grown an infatuation with a true crime case. Sofia never tried to speak to her about Twin Peaks. So, for now, she only kept a picture of Hue along with a short description of him and what they'd been through. She fought with herself about how to immortalize him in her notebook. Every time she started a sentence, she'd erase it only to do the same with the next one. It wasn't until she took a deep breath and told herself to wing it, that she was finally satisfied. Under his picture, she wrote:

This man carried the weight of the world on his shoulders. And even though he had no reason to show love, he did so anyway.

She wasn't finished, but it was a good start. The only missing piece was Heather. Just like the little girl, Sofia never really knew her dad. All she saw was the amazing man she made him up to be, so over time, they slowly drifted apart. His social media photos, however, showed how busy he was partying each day. Yet, Sofia couldn't find any information about Heather. She knew the little one escaped Twin Peaks, but she was dying to know where she ended up. Did her soul go to rest after they defeated Dabria? Sofia sat in the glow of her computer screen and gave another sigh. With the school year ending, Sofia became desperate. Every student was required to complete a set of community service hours to meet their graduation requirements. This year, Sofia chose to volunteer at a foster home. She skimmed through all the kids' photos the organizer emailed her.

But as she read through the roster, one of the babies caught her attention. Her picture showed she had blonde hair, and the name tag on her crib said, "Heather." Sofia ran her fingers over the girl's face. Then, she rubbed her eyes after pulling away from the screen, thinking that this was just a trick. Heather died in Twin Peaks. Was it possible for her to even be in the real world? Sofia shook her head. *Whatever, they probably just share the same name.* Sofia let out a deep breath.

To her, the baby had to have been a coincidence, but since the lost souls who entered Twin Peaks were able to be reincarnated as animals when they became 'the saved,' was it possible to reincarnate as a different person?

"That's a big stretch," Sofia muttered to herself, but after seeing an entirely different world, anything was possible to her. For the time being, Sofia leaned back in her chair with Hue's scrapbook to ease her mind. "We did it," she said to his picture.